Note to Readers

While _____ attle
over v_____ en—
struggl_____ nited
States t

Sor _____ for
women _____ for
the righ _____ ding
minori _____ t an
amend _____ sed.

Aft _____ tood
firm. E _____ the
right t _____ the
end, th _____ uar-
anteed

WOMEN
WIN *the* VOTE

JoAnn A. Grote

PUBLISHING, INC.
Uhrichsville, Ohio

ISBN 1-57748-452-5

Published by Barbour Publishing, Inc.
P.O. Box 719
Uhrichsville, Ohio 44683
http://www.barbourbooks.com

Member of the
Evangelical Christian
Publishers Association

Printed in the United States of America.

Cover illustration by Peter Pagano.
Inside illustrations by Adam Wallenta.

CHAPTER 1

The Parade

"Here comes the parade from Minneapolis!" Gloria Allerton's blue eyes shone. "Do you see her?" she asked her twelve-year-old brother, Larry. "Do you see Mother?"

Larry tugged at the bill of the hat covering his strawberry-blond hair. "No, but she's in that crowd of yellow and black somewhere."

Their father laughed. "From the air, the city must look like a giant bumblebee. All those women seem to be dressed in the suffragists' yellow and black. There's yellow bunting on every car and hanging from windows on business buildings. Women are carrying yellow and black banners and wearing yellow

5

flowers. The city is mad with those colors!"

From his perch on Father's shoulders, seven-year-old Harry scowled down. "Where ith Mother?"

Harry was always saying *th* instead of *s* sounds since he lost his two front teeth.

"She's in that parade with the rest of the women from Minneapolis who fought for the right of women to vote," Father told him.

A band struck up the "Battle Hymn of the Republic." The women marching raised their voices in song. The people watching the parade began singing, too.

Larry groaned. "Battle Hymn of the Republic" was the theme song for the suffragists, women like his mother who were fighting for the right of women to vote in elections. Suffs, people called them for short.

"I've heard that song so many times that I could sing it in my sleep," Larry told Gloria.

She stopped singing long enough to grin impishly at him. "I think I've *heard* you singing it in your sleep."

He snorted and joined in with the singers.

When the song was over, the crowd cheered. Women on the lawn and sidewalks waved bright banners with the words "Votes for Women" and "Justice for Women."

Thousands of women from Minneapolis were walking or riding in cars in the parade. They were meeting a parade of St. Paul women in front of the state capitol in St. Paul. The Allerton family stood on the grounds of the huge building, excited to watch Mother be part of the celebration.

The women had a lot to celebrate. A little more than two weeks earlier, the United States legislature had passed the Nineteenth Amendment. It gave women the right to vote in any election. Mother had been working with other suffs for that right most of her life.

"Wa–a–a–aw!" A wail pierced the noise of the crowd.

At the sound, Gloria leaned forward and picked up a baby from the buggy in front of them. "Poor Freddie," she cooed. "Does all the noise frighten you?"

"Noise can't scare him," Larry scoffed. "He's the noisiest thing around."

Gloria put Fred against her shoulder and patted his back. She glared at Larry. "You'd be noisy, too, if you were only a month old and couldn't talk to people. How else is he supposed to get our attention?"

Larry ignored the question.

"Hey!" Gloria slapped a hand to the top of her bobbed brown hair. "It's raining again!"

Larry laughed at the sight of a raindrop rolling down over Gloria's forehead and along her nose.

"Quit laughing and put up the umbrellas," she ordered.

"You can't boss me around. I'm two years older than you are."

"Larry, hurry! My hair is going to look awful if it gets rained on."

Father cleared his throat. "Put up the umbrellas, Larry."

Larry did as he was told, holding one large, black umbrella over himself, Gloria, and Fred and another over the baby carriage so it wouldn't get soaked. Father was holding a large umbrella over himself and Harry, who was still perched on his shoulders.

Father winked at Larry. "I'm surprised your mother didn't have yellow and black umbrellas made up for today, just in case it rained."

Larry and Gloria laughed.

Harry giggled. "The rain thoundth like drumth."

He's right, Larry thought, *the rain on the umbrellas does sound like drums. It's really coming down hard.*

The rain didn't dampen the enthusiasm of the women marching. They all wore huge grins.

"Hey!" Father squeezed one of Harry's legs. "Stop leaning on my straw hat, Harry. You'll break the brim."

Harry giggled and pushed at the brim with both hands.

"Hold the umbrella, Harry," Father said.

When Harry grabbed the umbrella, Father reached up and took Harry down from his shoulders, then took the umbrella back.

"But I want to thee," Harry wailed.

"I told you to stop ruining my hat. Besides, you're getting too big to sit on my shoulders."

Harry tugged at Larry's arm. "Can I sit on your shoulders? You're big."

"No. Watch the parade."

Harry stood on tiptoe and tried to see over the heads of the people in front of them.

"Hey, there's Mother!" Larry pointed toward the parade.

"Where?" Father asked.

"Where?" Harry asked, jumping up and down. "I can't thee!"

"Hey! Put the umbrella back up, Larry!" Gloria tried to cover her head with one hand and hold Fred with the other. "It's not a pointer!"

"Can we share your umbrella, buddy?" an older male voice asked.

Larry turned in surprise. "Greg! Sure, take this one."

Greg was the older brother of Larry's best friend, Jack. Greg looked a lot like Jack, with long brown hair and a lop-sided smile, but he was ten years older than Jack and Larry.

After Larry handed an umbrella to Greg, he quickly stepped under the umbrella that sheltered Father and Harry. The other umbrella still covered Gloria, Fred, and part of the baby buggy.

Larry remembered that it had only been a month ago that

he and all of Minneapolis and St. Paul had been watching Greg and the rest of 151st Rainbow Division parade by when they returned from the war. He chuckled. He hadn't thought then that he and the rest of the Twin Cities would ever be out watching his mother parade past! But here it was, June 9, and that's exactly what they were doing. Larry wondered what other surprises the year 1919 had in store for his family.

Another young man about Greg's age was sharing Greg's umbrella. Larry glanced at him curiously. He didn't know him. The man had long blond hair brushed back in the popular style. Right now it was wet from the rain.

"This is my friend, Luke Harding," Greg told Larry. He introduced the Allerton family to Luke. "Luke was a pilot in the war."

"A pilot!" Larry's heart started beating so loudly he thought surely Greg and Luke must hear it. "Were you ever shot down?"

"Lawrence!" Father scowled down at him.

Larry pushed his free hand into his trousers pocket. Father must have thought that wasn't a proper question.

"I don't mind his asking," Luke told Father. He smiled at Larry. His gray eyes were friendly. "No, my plane was never shot down, but it was hit a few times."

"Did you shoot any of the old Kaiser's planes down?"

"Lawrence!" Father thundered again.

Luke laughed. "A few. And I wounded a few more of his buses."

"Buses?" Gloria's forehead crinkled as she looked up at him, puzzled.

Luke shrugged. "That's what a lot of pilots call the planes."

"Are you from Minneapolis?" Gloria asked. "Were you in the parade last month with Greg, when we watched the soldiers who came home from the war?"

9

"I'm from Chicago," Luke said. "I wasn't in the Minneapolis parade, but I was in a parade in Chicago."

"Our mother is in this parade." Gloria smiled at him over the top of sleeping Freddie's head.

Greg nodded. "She and the other suffs deserve a parade. I'm glad Congress finally passed the law giving women the right to vote. They deserve it after all they did to help win the war."

"I'll say!" Luke agreed. "There were nurses on the front lines helping wounded men while bullets were flying all around them. If women are willing to risk their lives for their country, they should be able to vote for the people who make the country's laws."

Gloria beamed.

Larry was glad these two men who had fought in the war were proud of his mother and other women like her.

Greg shifted the brim of his hat lower over his forehead. Larry thought he saw a sad look come into Greg's eyes.

Then he remembered. Violet, the girl Greg was going to marry, had been a nurse. She'd worked with the soldiers at the hospital at Fort Snelling in St. Paul. She'd caught the flu from the soldiers and died last winter while Greg was fighting in France.

Sadness crept into Larry's heart, too. That had been a scary time, with the war killing people in Europe and the flu killing people at home.

The war and the flu are over now, he told himself, straightening his shoulders beneath his white shirt. *There's nothing to be afraid of anymore.*

Gloria placed sleeping Freddie in his buggy and straightened up again.

"Wa. . .a. . .aw!"

Gloria groaned. Her shoulders sagged. "He's getting heavy."

"I'll hold him." Father picked him up. After a few sobs, Fred fell asleep again against Father's suit-covered shoulder.

The mayor of St. Paul and some of the other city and suffragist leaders were on the steps of the huge capitol. The crowd quieted enough to hear them give speeches. They told of the long fight to win the vote for women. Often the speakers had to stop while the crowd cheered and waved banners.

While the people were speaking, Mother joined the family. She slipped under the umbrella with Father. He winked down at her, and she gave him a wide grin, her eyes sparkling.

"You shouldn't need an umbrella," Larry told her. "That big hat of yours will keep off the rain!"

Two large yellow silk roses were pinned to the black band above the wide hat brim.

Mother and Father laughed at his joke.

When the speakers were done, the Allertons joined the rest of the crowd making their way toward the trolley cars that would carry them back across the river to Minneapolis.

Father smiled at Mother. "I'm proud of you and happy for you, too. But I'm also glad that you'll have more time to spend at home now that Congress passed the amendment. What with the meetings, rallies, and fund-raisers the suffs have held, together with your war work and the flu epidemic and the new baby, we've hardly seen each other the last year or so."

"Oh, this isn't the end." Mother's eyes danced beneath the brim of her hat. "It's just the beginning."

Father stopped in his tracks. "The beginning!"

"Oh, yes. There's ever so much to be done."

"Like what?" Father asked.

"Yes, what?" Larry echoed.

"First," Mother put the gloved index finger of one hand against a gloved fingertip on the other hand, "we must convince the states to ratify the amendment. Even though Congress passed the amendment, it doesn't become law until three-fourths of the states agree that it will be law, you know."

Father nodded. "What else is there to be done?"

"Why, we must teach women to be wise voters."

Gloria grinned and nodded. She'd gone to many suffragist meetings with her mother. Larry knew that if she were old enough, she would have been in the parade, too.

Father gave a huge sigh. "Here, Larry." He handed Fred to him. "You and I may as well get used to watching the boys while the women watch the politicians."

Larry laughed along with Gloria and Mother. It was quite a joke to think he was going to be turned into a babysitter while Gloria learned how to vote!

CHAPTER 2
The Barnstormers

It wasn't a joke after all, Larry thought on a day in late August, remembering his father's words almost three months later.

He dropped into a wooden chair beside the kitchen table, crossed his arms over his chest, and glared at Harry. The younger boy was working on a poster at the table. The tip of his tongue stuck out from between his lips while he concentrated. Fred lay in his bassinet nearby.

"Why do I always have to be the one to watch Harry and

13

Fred?" Larry asked his mother. "Gloria is always going to suff meetings with you. Why can't she stay home and watch the boys for a change?"

Mother put a clean linen rag over the cookies in a basket. "They aren't called suffragist meetings any longer," she reminded him.

"We go to League of Women Voters meetings now," Gloria said with a proud little lift of her chin.

"Aw, who cares what they're called? I still think Gloria should have to watch the boys more often."

A guilty feeling wormed its way through him. Gloria did her share of watching Harry and Fred. Sometimes at the meetings they went to, Gloria had to watch not only their brothers but other children as well.

"It isn't always so bad," Gloria said. "Didn't you go to the State Fair with us a couple days ago?"

"Yes," he agreed angrily, "and helped you and Mother work at the League of Women Voters booth, handing out flyers, when I wasn't watching Harry and Fred."

"Oh." Gloria's eyebrows raised and she looked at him in pretend surprise. "I thought you and Jack spent a lot of time visiting exhibits and eating treats and playing games and watching the barnstormers."

Larry felt his cheeks grow warm. "Not as much time as we wanted to spend."

Gloria's comment reminded him of the barnstormers he and Jack planned to see that afternoon. He was sure Mother wouldn't want him to bring little Fred to the field to watch fearless pilots!

"Now, children," Mother said.

Larry hated when she called them children!

Mother patted his shoulder. "I think it's important for Gloria to learn everything she can about how to be a good citizen. That way when she's an adult, she can make wise choices when she votes."

Larry spread his hands. "But Jack and I had plans for this afternoon."

"Take your brothers along," Mother suggested.

"Fred gets awful heavy after awhile."

"Use the baby carriage," Mother said.

Larry sat up straight. Didn't mothers know anything at all about what it's like to be a boy? "Aw, Mother! Guys don't push baby buggies. Not unless they want the other guys to call them a sissy."

Mother shrugged. "Have it your own way. Whatever you decide, you must watch your brothers."

She leaned over Harry's shoulder. "The poster looks very good, Harry. Thank you for helping. Gloria and I will take the poster with us to our meeting."

Ratify Number 19, the poster said. Gloria had helped Harry with it, since he didn't know how to spell well yet.

He probably doesn't even know that the poster means they want Minnesota's leaders to agree that the Nineteenth Amendment will be a law, Larry thought.

Larry tried one more time to get out of babysitting. "Minnesota passed their own law in March saying women can vote. I don't see why you and Gloria can't stay home now. What does it matter whether Minnesota ratifies the old Susan B. Anthony Amendment?"

Mother pulled a broad-brimmed hat over her bobbed hair. "You know very well, Lawrence Allerton, that the antisuffrage people are trying to convince our legislators not to ratify the amendment. It's important that as many states as possible ratify it. I'm afraid not all states will agree it should be law. What if one less state voted not to make it law? All our work for the women in the country would be lost. We must see that

Minnesota ratifies the amendment to support our poor sisters in those states that aren't wise enough to give them a vote."

Larry gave up.

Mother set a stack of small papers in front of him. "Here are some flyers. If you decide to go with Jack, you can hand these flyers out."

He glanced at the rectangular papers. "Every woman a voter in 1920," he read.

He sat scowling while Mother and Gloria prepared to leave with their posters and cookie basket.

When Gloria followed Mother through the swinging door into the hall, she looked back over her shoulder and wrinkled her nose at Larry.

"She doesn't have to rub it in," he muttered. He pushed the chair back. It scraped on the linoleum. "Come on, Harry. Let's get Fred ready. Jack's waiting for us."

They took a trolley to get toward the edge of the city, where Greg had told them Luke Harding was barnstorming. Larry had to do some fast talking before the driver let him bring the red wooden wagon on the trolley. "Better than a baby buggy," Larry told Jack.

His heart raced as it always did when they neared the field where people were gathered watching the barnstormers. The wagon bounced along behind him as they hurried down the dirt road. Larry had padded the wagon bed well with blankets to protect Fred.

Men and women of all ages as well as children lined the edge of the field. Their heads were tilted toward the sky, where a plane with two wings on each side of the two cockpits was framed against the graying sky.

"A lot of clouds have rolled in since we left home," Larry told Jack. "If it rains, they'll stop flying."

Larry pulled the bill of his hat down over his eyes to watch

Luke's biplane come in for a landing.

The hay bent in front of the plane. When the wheels touched the ground, the plane rattled across the field toward the crowd. Luke spun the plane about to keep the dangerous propellers away from the people. When he turned off the engine, the propeller made a clack-clack sound as the plane slowed to a stop.

Luke climbed out of his cockpit. He was wearing a waist-length jacket. His goggles were pushed up on his leather helmet. He helped a middle-aged man out of the front cockpit and onto the bottom wing. From there the man slid to the ground. He wore a big grin. He grabbed one of Luke's hands with both of his and shook it heartily. Luke grinned back at him.

The man ran across the field toward the crowd, waving one arm in the air. "It was great, Bertha! Simply great! Aren't you goin' to try her?"

"I should say not!" a tall, skinny woman beside Larry declared. "Why, it's a miracle you didn't fall right out of that thing and land on your head in the field."

The man came to a stop in front of her, laughing. "Oh, Bertha. Who knows when you'll have another chance? And it only costs a penny a pound."

Bertha clamped her arms over her chest. "As if I'm going to let you know how much I weigh!"

"Jack! Larry! Hello!"

Larry returned Luke's wave. Larry thought his shirt buttons would pop off, he was so proud. Luke not only remembered them from the parade last June, but he called to them in front of everyone!

Larry and Jack had watched a lot of barnstormers that summer, but they hadn't seen Luke since June. He'd left Minneapolis to travel elsewhere with his machine soon after the suffs' parade.

The boys sat down in the hay, which had been trampled by

the crowds, and watched the planes. The hay poked through their trousers and itched a bit, but they ignored the discomfort. The two pilots flew about a dozen people each, but it took a long time. There was only room for one pilot and one passenger in each plane. Larry didn't mind; the longer the show lasted, the better! Each ride lasted about ten minutes.

After a couple hours, Luke came jogging across the field toward them. The unhooked straps of his leather helmet swung as he ran. In one hand he carried a fuel tin.

"I saw your wagon," he said, "and wondered if you'd get me some gas for the bus. I only have enough fuel for a few more rides. There's a station down this road about a mile. I saw it from the air."

Larry was pleased as punch to be asked, but he didn't know if he could help. "I. . .I have to watch my brothers."

"I'll go," Jack offered, jumping to his feet.

"Thanks!" Luke grinned. "I'll give both of you a ride later in return for the favor."

Larry and Jack grinned at each other. This was better than anything Larry had hoped for!

A man in a business suit and hat poked Luke in the shoulder. "You taking any more passengers up today?"

"Sure!" Luke answered. "Are you looking for a ride?"

The man nodded soberly. "I'd like to see what my house and business look like from the air." He held up a heavy camera. "Think I can take a picture from your airplane?"

"You can, but you'll need to be careful not to drop it over the side when you take the picture. It's windier than you think up there. You might want to leave your hat down here with a friend, too. It'll blow away if it's not tied on."

"I'll watch it for you," Larry said.

"Thanks, son." The man handed it over.

Luke and the businessman headed toward the plane.

Larry picked up Fred from the wagon, and Harry spread Fred's blankets on the bent hay. Then Larry put Fred down on the blankets. Fred wiggled and squinted.

"Too much sun for you?" Larry asked. "Seems cloudy to me, but maybe it is too bright for you." He yanked the wide brim of Fred's blue bonnet over the baby's eyes. "Don't know why boy babies have to wear these girly-looking hats. You need a hat like mine."

Jack set the tin can in the wagon. The wagon wheels jangled as Jack started off with the wagon at a run.

Harry flopped down on the blanket beside Fred. Larry knelt beside them. "Good idea, Harry. The blanket isn't nearly as itchy as the hay."

It couldn't have been more than half an hour before Jack came back with the gas. Luke was pouring it into the plane when the rain started.

"Oh, no." Disappointment flooded Larry. "Now we won't get our rides."

CHAPTER 3
The Plane Ride

People ran from the field. Some headed for their cars. Those who had walked raced down the dirt road toward the city.

Larry threw Fred's blankets around him and put the baby into the wagon.

"Over here!" Luke called.

Larry looked up. Luke was motioning him with his arm. "Get under the wing!"

"Come on, Harry!" Larry headed toward the plane, pulling Fred in the wagon behind him. Jack and Harry raced in front of him.

Luke headed toward a corner of the field and soon returned with a tarp, a bedroll, and a tin set of cooking utensils like soldiers used. "Give me a hand with this tarp, will you, boys?"

Larry and Jack scurried out from under the shelter of the wing to help Luke tie the tarp over the cockpit areas of the plane. At least the seating area and wooden instruments and instrument panel were protected from the rain.

"Shouldn't the Jenny be in a hangar?" Larry asked when they were back under the wing. It wasn't windy, so the wing kept most of the rain off them.

"A shower like this won't hurt her," Luke answered, pulling off his leather flying gloves, "but I wouldn't want her out in a field during a storm with strong winds, lightning, or hail. Large hail can go right through the fabric."

Like most planes, Luke's Jenny was made of wood, wire, and canvas. Larry could see where a number of patches had already repaired holes in the fabric.

The sides of the plane were dirty and oil streaked, but Larry thought it looked great. He could imagine himself in a helmet and goggles, flying it one day!

Luke pulled off his soft leather helmet and shook out his straight blond hair.

Harry scrunched up his face and looked at Luke. "Ith Jenny the name of your plane?"

Larry didn't wait for Luke to answer. "All planes of this type are called Jenny."

"That's right," Luke told Harry.

Larry couldn't resist showing off a bit more of his knowledge. "Jennies are about twenty-seven feet long. Their wings span about forty-three-and-a-half feet. There's a ninety-horsepower engine, and it can fly about seventy-five miles an hour, tops."

Luke laughed. "That's right, unless the bus is in a nosedive. You must like airplanes to know so much about the Jennies."

Jack groaned. "He reads everything he can get his hands on about airplanes."

21

"I want to fly one day," Larry told Luke.

"Then I'm sure you will."

Larry touched the side of the airplane, touched it softly like it was something very special. "It was a Jenny the pilot flew in the first flight over the Canadian Rockies this year, wasn't it?"

"That it was." Luke turned back to Harry. "I named this plane *Josephine,* after a special lady I once knew. See her name painted on the nose of the plane?"

Harry looked where Luke pointed and nodded. "Ith that the Jothephine in the thong?" He started singing. "'Come Jothephine in my flying machine. Up we go. Up we go!'" He raised his arms over his head on the word *up.*

Luke laughed. "No, not the same lady. But that's a good song, don't you think?"

Harry nodded. "It'th one of my favoriteth."

"He likes the 'Up we go!' part," Larry said.

"Yeth!" Harry grinned.

Luke laughed. "Me, too, buddy."

"Did you get *Josephine* from the United States Air Service?" Jack asked.

Luke nodded. "After the war, there were a lot of extra planes, so the air service and army have sold many to ex-air service pilots like me."

"Are the holes in *Josephine* from hail or from bullets?" Larry asked.

"Both." Luke looked grim.

A thrill ran along Larry's arms. He tried to imagine what it must have been like up in the air with only a little fabric and wood between Luke and the enemy's bullets.

Harry's brown eyes grew large. "Did people shoot at you, Luke?"

"In the war they did."

"Weren't you thcared?"

"I sure was, buddy." Luke bent forward, placed his hands on his knees, and looked closely at Harry. "Is that a missing-teeth lisp I hear?"

Harry grinned and pointed to the space that used to hold his two front teeth. "They're coming back, though."

Luke nodded gravely. He glanced at Larry. "Looks like you boys will have to wait until better weather for your ride. Don't worry. I won't forget my promise."

Hope lifted Larry's spirits. "Are you going to be around Minneapolis for a few days?"

"Yes. I'll use this field for a while longer if the farmer lets me. It's so close to the city that a lot of riders can find me."

"Will you fly tomorrow?" Larry asked hopefully.

"That depends on the rain. If the field is muddy, it will be difficult to taxi and take off and land." Luke squinted through the rain at a fenced pasture beside the field. "Have to remind the farmer to keep those cows away from this field, though. Can't have them eating my plane."

"Eating your plane!" Harry burst out laughing.

"I'm serious. Cows like to eat the fabric."

Fred let out a wail.

Luke squatted beside the wagon and reached for the baby. "What's wrong, little fella?" He lifted Fred up, started to hold him close, then held him out at arm's length and laughed. "Guess we know what your problem is. Do you have a clean diaper along, Larry?"

Harry held his nose.

"Phew!" Jack's face looked like he'd bitten into a lemon.

Larry pulled a clean diaper from the blankets. His face burned. This would have to happen when Luke picked Fred up! Why, oh why, hadn't Mother made Gloria take care of Fred?

Two sunny days later, Larry and Jack returned to the field.

Larry could hardly stand the excitement. As they went through the gate in the fence and into the field, he grabbed Jack's arm. "Just think, we get to fly today for the first time!"

It was only ten in the morning, so there wasn't a crowd gathered at the field yet. "Most of the people come during their lunchtimes and in the early evening after work," Luke told them.

He was working on his engine.

"Is something wrong with the plane?" Larry asked uneasily. *Are we going to miss out on our promised rides again?* he wondered.

"Nope. Just tightening some screws. Have to keep a plane in tip-top shape if you want it to be safe, and I want *Josephine* here to be as safe as possible when there's air between her and the ground."

"Where's your friend?" Jack asked.

"The other pilot?" Luke asked. "Flew off to another town." He grinned down at them. "Most barnstormers don't like staying in one place too long. We get restless."

He jumped down and put his wrench in a small metal toolbox. "A barnstormer has to be a mechanic as well as a flyer."

Larry handed him a newspaper. "I brought this for you. There's an article that says for the first time flights are being scheduled every day between London and Paris. Thought you might want to read about it."

"Thanks!" Luke wiped his hands off on a dirty rag and took the newspaper.

Jack held up a large white handkerchief tied in a knot and a bottle of milk. "We brought you some food, too. Some roast beef and bread from my mom."

"And some cookies," Larry added.

"That will taste great after your rides," Luke said, thanking them with a smile.

He glanced over the article. "Guess it was only a matter of time before someone decided to make money flying people between those two cities. They learned in the Great War that planes could fly over the channel."

"It would be kind of scary to fly over ocean water like that," Larry said, "but it would be fun, too!"

"Huh! Says you!" Jack shivered. "I wouldn't want to try it."

"It can be pretty scary," Luke admitted. "British fighting pilots started crossing the English Channel five years ago when the war in Europe started. They were ordered to ram into any German Zeppelin airships they saw over the channel."

"*Ram* them?" Jack asked. "Not shoot them down?"

"Ram them," Luke said. "A scary idea, since they didn't have parachutes back then. In case the pilots fell into the water, they wore inner tubes from car tires around their waists." Luke shook his head. "Those were some pretty brave men. There have been lots of improvements in air travel since then, thanks to the war."

"I would have fought on the ground with the army instead of in the air!" Jack said firmly.

Larry laughed. He knew flying was dangerous, but it looked so exciting! "I can't understand why anyone wouldn't want to fly."

"I want to fly," Jack insisted. "That is, I want to take a ride and see what it's like. But I wouldn't want to be in the air with people shooting at me!"

Larry could understand that.

"It's been a great year for flying," Luke said. "In June, two Englishmen flew nonstop across the Atlantic from Newfoundland to Ireland. Did you hear about that?"

The boys nodded.

"I read about that," Larry said. "The pilots flew a little over nineteen hundred miles in just over sixteen hours!"

"Don't forget, when they landed, they crashed the plane in an Irish bog," Jack added.

Larry remembered seeing a picture of the biplane, its nose crumpled into the bog, its tail stuck in the air.

"One day, someone will make it across the widest part of the Atlantic nonstop," Luke said. "Mark my words."

Larry grinned. "That would be quite a ride."

"Speaking of rides," Luke said, "which of you wants to go up first?"

"I'll go!" Larry volunteered.

"This your first time?" Luke asked.

Larry nodded. He was too excited to speak.

Luke took his bedroll and tin cook set from the back cockpit and asked Jack to put them at the side of the field. Then he handed Larry an extra helmet and goggles. "You'll find wearing these more comfortable in the wind than going without."

Larry slid the tight helmet over his head and fastened it securely beneath his chin, copying Luke. Then he slid the goggles over the helmet, resting them on his forehead like he'd seen pilots do in pictures.

"You'll be riding in the front cockpit," Luke explained. "Since this was a training plane, there are controls in both the front and back cockpits. I'll show you how to throw a switch so I can start the propeller."

"I'll turn the prop for you," Jack offered.

"Thanks, but that's too dangerous."

Luke helped Larry into the open cockpit. After his seat belt was fastened, Luke showed him which switch to flip. "Once I've given the propeller two complete turns, I'll stand back and yell, 'Contact.' That's when you throw the switch. Got that?"

Larry nodded.

"Then I'll grab the blade and whirl the propeller. That will start the motor. Throttle it this way but not a lot. Just enough to make sure the motor doesn't quit. Then I'll climb into the back cockpit and take over."

Luke jumped down, ducked under the double wing, and headed toward the front of the plane.

Larry watched the propeller over the nose of the plane. Once it went around. Larry's fingers closed over the switch. Twice the propeller circled.

"Contact!"

Larry threw the switch.

The roar of the engine almost made him jump out of his seat. He hadn't known it would sound so loud from the cockpit! The noise almost made him forget to work the throttle, but he remembered in time. This was almost like being a real pilot.

Luke climbed up on the bottom wing. "Good job!" he called over the motor's roar. "When we're flying, don't touch any of the controls." He pointed at a stick. "You'll probably see the stick move, but don't worry. It will be moving because I'm moving my stick. That controls the nose and wings."

Luke slipped into the back cockpit. A moment later, the engine grew louder as he gave it more power. They rolled over the field.

Larry bounced about in the small cockpit as the plane bumped over the hay-covered lands. Then the wooden stick moved backward, and suddenly they were soaring up.

The wind caught his breath away. He blinked his eyes against the force of it. Tears sprang to his eyes. Then he remembered his goggles and pulled them down over his eyes. Now he could see!

They seemed to zoom toward the clouds. His chest felt thick with excitement mixed with fear.

The stick on the floor moved forward. The little plane stopped climbing and leveled off. Larry tried to see the ground, but it wasn't easy with the bottom wing between him and land.

He could see glimpses of Minneapolis's buildings in front of the wing. They looked like toys! His stomach did a flip-flop when he saw how high they were in the plane. Then he forgot his fear in trying to see as much as he could.

Luke circled the plane above a three-story building. The plane tipped sideways a bit when he circled, and Larry could see better. *Why, that's my school!* he realized. When they'd gone past it, he turned and grinned at Luke to show him he liked what he'd seen.

Soon Luke circled again. Larry saw his house and Jack's below. Cars and people on the street looked too small to be real. Was that Gloria and Harry playing with a red wagon? He waved, just in case someone he knew was watching the plane buzzing overhead. Wouldn't Gloria and Harry be surprised when he told them later that he'd seen them from the air!

Wonder flooded through Larry as they flew. It was like something Tom Swift might be doing, flying over the city.

Luke flew over the downtown area. Buildings that had seemed tall when Larry was on the ground were short and small below them. Next they circled St. Anthony Falls on the Mississippi River. Larry liked that best of all. The white water that plunged over the falls created a huge white spray in the black band of the river.

Disappointment took away a bit of his excitement when Larry saw they were nearing the field and would soon be landing. Still, he'd had a longer ride than most of Luke's paying customers.

The land came toward them so fast that Larry caught his breath. Then he relaxed, remembering that Luke was a good pilot.

He heard the wind in the struts, the wooden slats between the wings. Cornstalks waved as they flew low over them, heading for the field where they'd started. The low-cut hay swished as the wheels swung through it. Then they were taxiing toward Jack, bouncing across the rough land.

Luke swung *Josephine* around, facing the plane away from Jack, and turned off the engine. The propeller slowed with a soft clack-clack sound.

A bit sad the ride was over, Larry unhooked his safety belt. Luke helped him over the cowl of the cockpit and onto the bottom wing. By the time Larry had slid to the ground, Jack was coming around the corner of the wing, sticking his slingshot into his back pocket.

"How was it?" Jack asked.

"Great! Simply tops!"

Luke smiled. "Glad you liked it."

"It felt. . ." Larry struggled to find the right words. "I felt free."

Luke's smile grew wider. "You're a born flyer, all right."

"Thanks for taking me up, Luke. It's just the best thing that's happened to me in my whole life is all!"

Luke bopped him lightly on the shoulder and winked. Then he turned to Jack. "Ready for your turn, buddy?"

Jack took a deep breath. Then he nodded.

"You'll like it. I know you will," Larry told him.

He took off his goggles and helmet and handed them to Jack. "Don't forget to put the goggles down over your eyes before the plane takes off," he warned him, "or you'll be crying like a baby."

Larry moved back near the fence, where it was safer, to watch the plane take off. He fought off feelings of jealousy. He wished he were going up again!

There were more people at the field, watching and waiting for their turn to fly. At the side of the dirt road were a couple black family cars, a tall delivery truck, and a snappy, low-cut roadster.

Even the fancy car didn't take Larry's attention from the plane. He watched it take off, imagining himself in it again.

When the plane was only a dot in the sky, he lay on his back in the sharp, low hay and chewed on the end of a hay stem while watching the clouds cross the blue sky.

I was up there, he thought, wonder coursing through him. *My life will never be the same again.*

CHAPTER 4

An Important Vote

"Gloria has all the fun." Larry tightened the belt about his schoolbooks with an angry jerk. It rocked the glass of milk sitting on the breakfast table.

Mother laughed at him, her eyes dancing. "Is that so? What about the airplane ride you took last week?"

"Yes, what about that?" Gloria's blue eyes challenged him. She was wearing what Larry called her "Little Mother" look again.

"That's different," he grumbled. A thrill ran through him, though. For a minute he felt sorry for his sister. Nothing could compare with flying!

Still, he wasn't going to agree with Mother. After all, a

guy had to stick up for his rights. That's what the women did, wasn't it?

"We weren't back in school then," he reminded Mother and Gloria. "I didn't get a day off school to go flying."

"Planes can fly any day of the week." Gloria smoothed a brush over her short dark bob. "The Minnesota government doesn't meet every day."

Father picked up Gloria's argument. "You know very well, Larry, that the governor has called a special session of the Minnesota legislature to ratify the Nineteenth Amendment. They are voting on it today. The governor has invited members of the Minnesota Woman's Suffrage Association to sit on the Senate floor during the vote. You can't expect Mother to ignore that invitation, not after all the years of work she's put into earning women the right to vote!"

"Gloria isn't Mother."

Mother picked up the half-empty milk glass from beside him. "She's worked hard for the vote, just the same. This is a very important time in history for American women. When Gloria is an old woman, I want her to be able to tell her grand-children she was there when the legislature ratified the Susan B. Anthony Amendment."

Harry looked up at her, his large brown eyes serious. Both hands were clenched about his milk glass. "Don't you want me to tell my grandchildren I wath there?"

Larry laughed. "Yes, Mother, don't you want us to all tell our grandchildren we were there?" Larry couldn't imagine being old and having grandchildren!

"Most men have been able to vote since the beginning of the country," Mother told him. "Black men and American Indians have been able to vote for years. Women have been fighting for this right since the country was founded. John Adams's wife wanted him to insist that the phrase 'all men are created equal' in the Declaration of Independence be changed to 'all women are created equal.' "

Father smiled at her. "If I were a legislator, I wouldn't dare vote against ratifying the amendment. After all, in Minnesota, women have the right to vote whether this becomes a federal law or not. If the legislators don't vote for it, I expect the women in Minnesota will vote the legislators out of office next election."

Mother nodded, her eyes sparkling. "I expect you are right."

Larry sighed. He knew he wasn't going to win his argument and get to stay home from school.

I'm glad I wore my best dress, Gloria thought, crossing the wide lawn in front of the capitol with her mother. Fashionably dressed women were all about them, crossing the wide lawn and walking up the marble steps.

Gloria ran one hand down the side of her dress's white skirt. She felt very grown-up in her new hat, a cloche. It had a high crown and a wide brim. Where the crown met the brim, she'd pinned the blue ribbon Harry had given her for her birthday a year ago.

The capitol wasn't very old. It stood on top of a hill, and a high dome crowned the center of the building.

Women and men filled the rotunda beneath the dome. The walls were limestone and marble, and the marble floor shone like new. It was one of the largest places Gloria had ever been inside. The beauty of the building and the important people she saw filled her with awe. She watched the people a bit shyly. She'd been excited to come, but now she felt a bit strange and out of place.

Mother pointed up. "Look at the ceiling."

Gloria bent back her head. The ceiling was the inside of the dome. A mural was painted on it. "Oh! It's beautiful!"

Gloria noticed a band getting organized in the middle of the rotunda. Their brass instruments gleamed. She and Mother walked around them, following the crowd of smiling women and serious men up a sweeping marble stairway to the Senate chamber.

Gloria knew many of the women entering the Senate chamber. Many of them were important and wealthy women, but they were friends of her and her mother. As more of the women they knew entered the large room and said hello to her and Mother, Gloria felt more comfortable.

It was the men with their sober faces and business suits that she watched wide-eyed. These were the senators, some of the most important men in the state. She didn't know any of them. They seemed bigger than life. Even though the room was crowded with people, Gloria edged closer to Mother.

"There's Uncle Erik!" she hissed in her mother's ear.

"He must be here to report on the vote for the *Tribune,*" Mother said. "Likely there are many other reporters here, too."

Gloria caught Uncle Erik's eye and waved. He grinned and waved back.

Noticing a strong smell of flowers, Gloria tore her eyes away from the interesting people! Bouquets of yellow flowers sat on the largest desk in the room between large pillars. Beneath that desk but still higher than most of the senators' desks was another desk. This long desk was also covered with bouquets of yellow flowers.

Every woman in the room had a yellow flower pinned to her hat or dress or both. Some of the flowers were real. Others were silk, like the one Gloria had pinned to the wide collar of her white dress.

"I'm so glad you let me come today," Gloria told Mother, "instead of making me go to school."

Mother smiled. "What could be more educational than seeing politics at work?"

Gloria pointed at the high desk. "Who sits there?"

"The most important senator," Mother said.

She'd barely finished saying so when the man climbed up and took his seat in a high-backed leather chair. Other men took places at the long desk.

A man stood at a podium in the middle of the long desk, raised his arms, and tried to get the people's attention. Senators took their seats, and soon everyone got quiet and waited for him to speak.

The man adjusted his glasses and looked over the crowded room. "The Nineteenth Amendment to the Constitution," he said in a very serious voice, "is being introduced to the Minnesota House of Representatives as we speak."

A roar went up from the women in the room. They waved large and small flags back and forth. The woman in front of Gloria waved her flag so hard that she knocked the wide yellow hat off the woman beside her.

Gloria laughed but pulled her own hat down a bit more tightly. She could feel the breeze from the flags.

The woman whose hat had been knocked off hurried to pick it up before anyone could step on it. Gloria thought she might be angry, but the woman laughed and put her hat back on.

The man held up his hands for silence. It took a few minutes for the room to quiet down again.

"As soon as the representatives have voted, they will send the results of the vote to the Senate," he said.

Cheers went up again. Applause filled the room.

Gloria tugged at her mother's sleeve. Mother bent her head toward her, still clapping. Gloria had to almost yell to be heard. "Do you think there is any chance the representatives won't ratify it?"

Mother shook her head, smiling. "The women in our groups have talked to most of the representatives. Most of the men have promised us they will vote for it."

After a few minutes, Gloria noticed a disturbance in the back of the room. A man was trying to get through the crowded aisle. Slowly people became aware of him and parted to let him through.

The room hushed as he climbed the steps and handed a paper to the senator seated in the high desk. Gloria held her breath as she watched the man put on his glasses and read the paper. When he was done, he removed his glasses and set them on the desk.

"Ladies and gentlemen," he began.

Everyone in the room leaned forward to hear him better.

"The Minnesota House of Representatives has ratified the Nineteenth Amendment to the Constitution of the United States."

The room erupted in cheers. Women jumped up and down. They hugged each other. Flags waved.

The senators looked at each other, shook their heads, and laughed.

Gloria jumped up and down, clapping. "I wish I'd brought a flag!" she called to Mother.

Gloria hadn't seen adults act this crazy since Armistice Day, when the war was over and they'd been singing and dancing through the streets. *And I thought politics was all serious and sober!* she thought.

The women quieted down when someone announced the governor would speak. He stood in the middle of the long desk behind the podium and spoke to the senators. He told them how important the amendment was to the country, how women had earned the right to vote by their hard and intelligent work during the war years, and how men needed women's help rebuilding the country after the war.

"Remember what President Wilson said," he told them. " 'Without women's counselings, we shall be only half wise.' "

"Hear, hear!" a senator called out.

The governor held up a hand. He picked up a paper. "I'm

sure there isn't a person in this room who doesn't know what the Nineteenth Amendment says, but the rules say to read it, so read it I will."

Laughter filled the air but died quickly away.

" 'The right of citizens of the United States to vote shall not be denied or abridged by the United States or by any state on account of sex.' "

After the governor read the amendment, the head senator gave instructions on voting.

Gloria's chest hurt from holding her breath when the voting began. She'd helped her mother work for this for a long time!

The name of each senator was called, and he gave his vote.

"Yea," the first senator called out.

One after another, the senators answered "Yea" to the question of how they voted on the amendment.

Some of the women cheered as the senators gave their votes. Others held hands and listened quietly, their eyes large. Some women dabbed at tears with lacy handkerchiefs.

When the votes were over, everyone knew the amendment had been ratified. Still, they waited for the head senator to say so. Gloria knew that the women had worked for the right to vote for so long that they wanted to hear the official announcement that Minnesota's legislature had passed the Susan B. Anthony Amendment.

"Ladies and Gentlemen, the Minnesota Senate has ratified the Nineteenth Amendment to the Constitution of the United States."

The room broke into more cheers and flag waving. Yellow flowers were tossed in the air. From the rotunda, the band Gloria had seen earlier broke into the "Battle Hymn of the Republic." Soon everyone in the chamber was singing.

The governor invited Clara Ueland to speak. Gloria and her mother knew Mrs. Ueland well. She had been at the head of the work for women's suffrage in Minnesota for years. Now everyone listened as she spoke of the long fight and what lay ahead for women.

Then she smiled at the senators. "In appreciation for your vote of confidence in the women of this state, we would like to invite you and the representatives to the St. Paul Hotel for dinner—a dinner which we suffragists shall serve to you."

Now it was the senators' turn to cheer.

On the steps of the capitol, Uncle Erik fell into step with them, notebook and pencil in hand. "That must be the fastest vote on record," he said with a grin. "It took the House and Senate together less than thirty minutes to ratify that amendment."

"Nonsense," Mother retorted. "It took them years and years. After all, women have been asking for the vote almost since the nation began."

Erik nodded, his eyes gleaming with laughter. "I guess you're right."

As they crossed the lawn, Mother said, "When you are old enough to vote, Gloria, be certain you take advantage of your right. Remember all the women who fought so that you might have a vote in choosing the men who make the laws you obey. Remember it is your responsibility to vote wisely for the men you want to make laws."

Gloria nodded. "I will remember and vote for the men, Mother." She grinned mischievously. "And for the *women* I want to make the laws."

CHAPTER 5
The Debate

"Tell me the truth," Larry demanded as they walked to school a few days later, "don't you get bored, Gloria, going to all those suffragist meetings with Mother?"

"Bored? I should say not!"

"Wouldn't you rather be playing than listening to women give speeches?" he asked.

He'd listened to a couple speeches over the years. It hadn't been so bad, but he wouldn't want to do it all the time like Gloria did.

"We do more than listen to speeches at the meetings," she told him. "We make clothes and quilts for war and flu orphans. We have bake sales and sell quilts to raise money for orphans and to educate women about voting. We make posters. We collect clothes and food and money for people in Europe who don't have anything because of the war. And—"

"Okay, okay, I get the idea." Larry held up both hands to stop her. "Still, wouldn't you rather be playing?"

She walked silently for a minute. It looked to Larry like she was thinking his question over.

"I guess," she started slowly, "it makes me feel good to think I'm helping other people. It makes me feel grown-up, too."

Larry nodded, swinging his books by his book belt. "I kind of felt that way when our Boy Scout troop helped with the war efforts and flu relief. But now I'm tired of it and glad the war and flu are over. I don't want to act like an adult anymore. I just want to have fun and forget the awful times!"

"I guess for me helping other people *is* fun."

Larry felt like squirming. He supposed he should feel guilty. Didn't the Bible say we were supposed to love our brother? *Jesus probably thinks Gloria is wonderful and that I'm selfish,* he thought, *but if I said I wanted to do anything but have fun, I'd be lying, and Christians aren't supposed to lie, either.*

When they reached the school, they split up and went to their own classes.

Gloria was all ears that morning when her teacher, Miss Colby, spoke of the Susan B. Anthony Amendment. She liked Miss Colby. The teacher was young and had been teaching only a couple years. Round, wire-rim glasses rested on her thin nose. She wore her thick brown hair wavy about her face and pulled the rest back in a bun. It looked so pretty that way that Gloria *almost*, but not quite, wished she hadn't cut her own hair in the popular bob.

"The United States Congress passed the amendment in June," Miss Colby told the class, "but so far only seventeen states have ratified it. Who can tell me how many states need to ratify it before it becomes a law?"

A number of hands shot up, including Gloria's.

"Yes, Ronald?" Miss Colby called on a stocky boy with bright red, curly hair and freckles.

"Three-fourths of the states have to ratify it."

"That's right," Miss Colby agreed. "Can you tell me how many states that is?"

"Well, there's forty-eight states, so three-fourths would be thirty-six."

"That's right."

Ronald always is good at arithmetic, Gloria thought. She was a bit slow at figuring sums in her head. She was much better at reading and history. Everyone knew Ronald was the smartest student in the class at arithmetic.

"Minnesota's legislature ratified the amendment earlier this month," Miss Colby said.

Gloria's hand shot into the air. "I was there at the capitol when they passed it, Miss Colby."

"Truly? Why don't you come up here and tell the class about it?"

Gloria walked to the front of the class. She wished she hadn't raised her hand. She didn't like speaking in front of everyone. Her fingers played with the sides of her red plaid jumper as she told what had happened in the Senate chamber. As she talked, she forgot to be nervous. Remembering that day, she became proud and excited all over again for what her mother and other women had won.

After lunch, she and her friend Mabel and some of the other girls were jumping rope in the schoolyard. Ronald came up and grabbed the rope right in the middle of Gloria's jump, tripping her. She stumbled to the ground.

"Hey! Stop it!" Gloria clutched at her knee, which she'd

scraped on the gravel of the schoolyard.

Ronald threw down the rope and sneered at her. "Think you're so smart, you and those suffs. Well, you're not. It will never pass, you know."

"What won't pass?" Gloria's knee hurt, and she tried to keep her tears from falling.

"The amendment. It won't be ratified by enough states."

"Will so!" Gloria struggled to her feet. Mabel grabbed her arm to help her.

"They will, too, ratify it," Mabel agreed, glaring at Ronald.

Ronald planted his fists on his hips and leaned forward, screwing his face into a mean look. "Won't! There are lots of states that won't ratify it, 'specially southern states. Down there they know how to keep a woman in her place!"

"Oh!" Gloria stomped her foot, furious. Then she winced at the pain in her knee.

"Children, children!" Miss Colby hurried over. "What is this argument about?"

Gloria told her. Ronald nodded.

"No one can tell what the states who haven't voted will do," Miss Colby told them. "Instead of fighting about it like street urchins, let's have the class debate it."

Ronald frowned. "Debate it? Like argue it for a grade?"

"Yes. We'll divide the class into teams. Each team will choose two students to be speakers for the debate. The rest of the teams will help with the research. The debate topic will be, 'Why the Nineteenth Amendment Should or Should Not Be Ratified.' "

When Miss Colby went back into the schoolhouse, Ronald gave Gloria's shoulder a shove. "Just like a woman to make a little argument into a lot of work!"

Gloria's hands balled into fists at her sides. "I wasn't the one to start the argument!"

The next morning, Miss Colby said, "I told the principal about the debate over the Susan B. Anthony Amendment. He thought it was a wonderful idea. He wants the debate to be given in the auditorium in front of the entire school." She beamed at the class.

Gloria dropped her head into her hands and groaned.

The team Gloria was on was to take the side that would argue the amendment *should* be ratified. When the team met for the first time, they immediately chose Gloria as one of the speakers.

"Oh, no!" She shook her head. "I don't like speaking in front of the class."

"But you're good at speaking," Mabel said. "And you know so much about women's suffrage after helping your mother and attending so many meetings with her."

The others nodded.

The other speaker the team chose was a quiet, studious boy named Arthur. He was very smart, and Gloria hoped he would do most of the speaking.

Gloria glared across the classroom at Ronald, who was meeting with the other group. "Let's work real hard on this," she said to her group. "I want to win!"

Over the next week, Gloria shared everything she knew with her team. They studied books in the library and talked to their parents about suffrage.

Gloria was surprised that some of the boys and girls in her group didn't think women should vote. Miss Colby hadn't asked whether they believed in suffrage or not before dividing the class into teams. Gloria was glad that at least everyone wanted to win, so they were working hard.

In addition to learning all they could about their side, the suff team made yellow and black posters. They even made handwritten flyers to hand out to other students.

The day of the debate, Gloria could hardly eat breakfast, she was so nervous.

"I don't think I can do this," she told Larry and Jack and Mabel as they walked to school together.

Larry put an arm around her shoulder. "Sure you can! Why, you probably know more about the reasons women should have a right to vote than anyone else in school."

"Larry's right," Mabel told her.

"But I'm so scared!"

Larry took Gloria's shoulders and turned her to face him. "Look," he said. "If you can't win a debate against Ronald for women getting the vote, I've been babysitting Harry and Fred the last couple years for nothing, and you owe me a lot!"

Gloria giggled, and some of her fear melted away.

"I mean it," Larry said. "I expect you to win today. If you don't, you owe me."

"Owe you what?" she asked, grinning.

He thought a moment. "The newest *Tom Swift* book, for one thing."

She looked at him in disbelief. *"One* thing? You mean there's more?"

He nodded. "You bet! Like letting me go watch the barnstormers while you watch Harry and Fred for a change."

"All right." She laughed and linked her arm with Mabel's. "I guess our team better win, Mabel."

When Gloria got up on stage later that day, she wasn't laughing anymore. Her stomach was doing flip-flops. Her hands were so sweaty that they made her notes wet.

She wasn't surprised to find Ronald was one of the speakers for the other team. She was glad he got to speak first rather than her.

Ronald walked to the middle of the stage and stood behind the podium, arranging his notes.

"The suffragists say men and women are created equal," he started. "Maybe they are equal, but they have different purposes to serve in this world. Men are meant to serve outside the home, in the world of work and politics. A woman's place is in the home, raising children who are healthy and teaching them what's right and wrong."

He went back to his seat on the opposite side of the stage from Gloria and Arthur.

It was Gloria's turn to go to the podium and respond to Ronald's argument. Her legs shook when she walked across the stage. When she laid her notes on the podium, the pages rattled. *I think I'm going to be sick,* she thought.

"Come on, Gloria! Give it to 'em good!" Larry's voice called out.

She bit back a giggle. It sounded like he was cheering at a football game! Soon other people started cheering for her.

She looked out over the crowd. Yellow and black banners waved. She wasn't alone. Her team was out there supporting her. *I can't let them down, no matter how scared I am,* she thought.

Gloria took a deep breath. Her voice shook when she began. "I agree with Ronald. The best thing women or a nation can do is raise its children well." She'd heard Clara Ueland say that once. "Mothers train their sons, the future voters, to make wise decisions. Why shouldn't the mothers who do the training also vote?"

The students who agreed with her cheered and whistled.

Gloria lost a little of her fear. "Again, I agree with Ronald. A woman's place is in the home, but it's not enough that she stay in the home. She has to care for her children's health and their morals. How can she control these things if she stays only in the home?

"A mother can clean house, but if the building is dirty, the streets aren't kept clean, and the garbage is not picked up, she can't protect her children from illness. She can cook food well, but if farmers and storekeepers can sell unclean food and milk, she can't buy good food for her family.

"It is the government of a city that makes laws about these things. The city's leaders do what they are told to do by the people who vote for them. Women don't elect the leaders, but women are held responsible for the things the leaders are in charge of.

"Women are by nature and training housekeepers. Let them help in the city housekeeping."

The audience clapped and whistled as Gloria walked back to her place.

Ronald's partner, a skinny girl named Martha spoke next.

"Why should women need to vote?" she asked, tossing her blond braids. "Don't they trust their husbands and fathers and brothers and sons to vote for the people and laws that are best for women and their families? Every woman who demands the right to vote is telling the men in her family that she doesn't trust them!"

Ronald and the students in the audience who agreed cheered as Martha returned to her seat. Gloria wondered whether Martha believed the anti's arguments or if she was just trying to get a good grade.

Arthur answered Martha's argument. "It's true, a woman's highest duty is to her family. But a man's highest duty is to his family, too. Would anyone suggest that a man would be a better father and more loyal husband if he didn't have the right to vote? Of course not! So why should the right to vote make a woman a worse mother and wife?"

Ronald strode back to the podium after Arthur sat down. "The average woman is no better educated than the average man. Allowing women to vote would mean there were more uneducated people voting for our leaders. All this comes from teaching girls to read!"

Ronald's team is using all the arguments we thought they would, Gloria thought, walking back to the center of the stage. *They're saying the same thing the anti's have been saying for years.* This realization made her even less afraid.

"Ronald is right again," she started. "Average men are allowed to vote. So why shouldn't average women be allowed the same right? Women are already schoolteachers, school officers and principals, librarians, members of library boards, police matrons, doctors, nurses, and lawyers. Aren't these women better educated than the average man? Shouldn't they have as much right to vote as the average man?"

Ronald's partner, Martha, spoke next. "If changes need to be made in our leaders or our laws, they don't need to be made by women voting. Instead, women should change public opinion and persuade their husbands. When public opinion changes, so will men's votes."

Arthur adjusted his glasses as he walked to the podium. "Both men and women have to obey the laws. Both men and women have to support the government. Both men and women have to suffer and sacrifice in times of war. Why shouldn't women be allowed to vote on the laws they are forced to follow and for the men who make those laws?"

When the debate was over, the principal came up on stage. "Both sides gave arguments we've heard from the adults in our city," he said. "Now we're going to give you students a chance to tell us who you think won this debate. We're going to have a school-wide vote."

The audience whistled and clapped.

Gloria bit her lip and shot a worried glance at Arthur. What if the students didn't vote for their team? Would all of their team get a poor grade?

CHAPTER 6

Airmail Arrives

All day Gloria worried. She couldn't concentrate on her class work. Even in history, one of her best subjects, she made a stupid mistake when Miss Colby called on her.

The day was almost over when the students' ballots had been counted and the principal came to their classroom to give them the result.

Gloria bit her bottom lip nervously when the tall, mustached man walked to the front of the room. What if she had to go home and tell her family that she had lost?

"First," the principal started, "I want to say that everyone did a fine job. I know that all of you who helped on both teams worked hard, not just the speakers. You are all to be congratulated."

Ronald raised his hand. "Does that mean that no matter which team wins the student vote, no one fails?"

The principal and Miss Colby laughed. Gloria couldn't see what was so funny.

"No one fails," Miss Colby said.

"In our country, someone always loses an election," the principal said, "but that doesn't mean the people who lose have failed. There is nothing dishonorable in fighting for what we believe is right."

Gloria relaxed against the back of her wooden chair. At least if her team lost, it wouldn't mean she and Arthur had made everyone on their team fail.

"The winning team is. . ." The principal paused, waiting for everyone's attention. "The suffragist side!"

Gloria sat straight up. "We won!" She beamed at Mabel, who grinned back at her.

"Hip-hip-hooray, Gloria!" her team cried. "Hip-hip-hooray, Arthur!"

Happiness swept through Gloria. After all her work and worry, they'd won. It had been worth it all.

She glanced to where Ronald was huddled in his chair, arms crossed over his chest. She could feel his anger all the way across the room.

There might not be anything dishonorable about standing up for what you believe, she thought, remembering the principal's words, *but it doesn't mean everyone will like you for it.*

She had the feeling she had made a very strong enemy.

Larry whistled as he walked into his classroom the next day. Ever since he'd arrived at school that morning, friends had been telling him what a great job his sister had done in the debate and that they'd voted for her team. He was so proud of her!

The first class of the day was history. Mr. Brown, the teacher, looked down his long, narrow nose and asked the class, "Who can tell me what the League of Nations is?"

That was easy. They'd been talking about that a lot. There was something about it in the newspaper almost every day. Larry lifted his hand and was called upon to answer.

"It's made up of people from many countries. Its purpose is to try to keep peace in the world so there won't be another Great War. President Wilson helped come up with the idea. He wants the United States to join, but Congress hasn't voted to join yet."

"That's correct." Mr. Brown took his spectacles from his vest pocket and put them on. "President Wilson is making a tour of the country, trying to convince people it is important for the United States to join the League of Nations. He hopes the people will convince Congress to join."

He snapped open a copy of the Minneapolis *Tribune*. "I'm going to read portions of speeches President Wilson has made on his tour. Then we will discuss what he has said."

He cleared his throat and began. " 'I would like to get together the boys who fought in the war,' " he quoted the president, " 'and I would stand up before them and say: Boys, I told you before you went across the seas that this was a war against wars, and I did my best to fulfill that promise. But I am obliged to come before you in humiliation and shame and say I have not been able to fulfill that promise. You are betrayed. You fought for something you did not get. And there will come a day in the vengeful Providence of God, another struggle in which not a few hundred thousand fine men from America will have to die, but as many million as

50

are necessary to accomplish the final freedom of the peoples of the world.' "

Mr. Brown turned the page. "In another town, the president said this: 'I can predict with absolute certainty that within another generation there will be another world war. . . . What the Germans used were toys compared with what will be used in the next war.' "

Frustration filled Larry's heart. Was it true? Hadn't the War to End All Wars put an end to wars? Would there really be another war that was worse than the Great War? Why wouldn't Congress vote to join the League of Nations and try to keep peace in the world? Had all the suffering of the war years been for nothing?

The rest of the class had the same questions as Larry, but they didn't have any answers.

"I wonder what Luke and your brother Greg will think of what the president said," Larry said to Jack on the way home. "Do you think they will feel cheated, after fighting in the Great War, when Congress won't join the League of Nations to help keep peace in the world?"

Jack dug his hands into his trouser pockets. "I don't know. Greg says after the horrors of the war, no soldier will ever see the world the same again. I don't know what Luke thinks, and we can't ask him."

"Why not?"

"He told Greg yesterday that he's leaving today. He's flying off toward the south, where it isn't so cold in the fall and winter. After all, he sleeps out under the wing of his plane a lot, you know. And he needs the warm weather to take riders up in his plane."

Luke, gone! Larry had come to think of him almost like an older brother. He was going to miss him terribly.

The next morning, Larry and the rest of the city received

more unpleasant news. President Wilson had collapsed on his tour. He was partially paralyzed.

Fall and winter went by slowly. The president's condition didn't improve much. At first he couldn't meet with other politicians, but he stayed on the job. Congress never did agree to join the League of Nations.

Gloria thought the most exciting time all winter was when their cousin Lydia married Donald Harrington right after Christmas. Lydia had met Donald at the military hospital at Fort Snelling, where she was a nurse.

Larry liked Lydia and Donald all right, but like he told Gloria, "I don't see why people make such a fuss about weddings."

Gloria had smiled, closed her eyes, and clasped her hands together. "Oh, weddings are so romantic! And Lydia's wedding dress was beautiful."

Larry snorted. "Who cares about romance? A wedding dress is just a dress. You know what's really beautiful? A biplane climbing against a cloudless blue sky. Now that's beauty!"

"Boys!" Gloria rolled her eyes and shook her head.

Larry didn't care. He'd take a biplane over a wedding dress any day.

To Larry it seemed he spent the entire winter waiting for spring and Luke's return. Whenever he wasn't in school or studying or watching his little brothers, he was either reading about airplanes and flying or building a wood and canvas model of Luke's *Josephine*.

Spring didn't bring Luke back to the city.

Larry and Jack still visited fields that summer with barnstorming pilots whenever they had the chance, but it wasn't the same without Luke. Still, Larry would have spent all his time around the barnstormers if he could!

He introduced himself to other barnstormers. He always

offered to run errands for them. Often he'd bring food from home for them. If the pilots were having a busy day, they wouldn't have much chance to eat. Sometimes he'd get a free ride in return. Sometimes the pilots would let him hang around after the other passengers left and watch while they tinkered with their engines.

Still, none of the pilots acted like true friends the way Luke had.

Larry's parents hadn't minded that he had taken Fred and Harry to the field the previous year, but this spring they'd changed their minds.

"No more," Father said. "It's too dangerous to have the small boys in the fields with the airplanes. You never know when there will be a crash. Besides, you can't keep your eyes on them every minute. What if one of them got in the way of a plane as it landed?"

Larry thought his parents were being foolish, but he knew better than to say so. Instead he built a small wooden airplane and placed it on the wheels of his old wagon. Fred loved to ride in it. Larry would pull him in it to the barnstormers' fields whenever he could manage to get away from the house without telling Mother and Father where he was going.

"If you want to keep seeing the barnstormers, you can't tell Mother and Father," he told Harry. "If you do, they won't let you come anymore."

"I can keep a secret," Harry assured him. He didn't lisp anymore now that his two front teeth had grown back.

June slipped by, then July.

Minneapolis and St. Paul agreed the two cities needed an airfield. Together, they started the Twin City Aero Corporation, and Jack's brother, Greg, went to work for the company. The company opened the Twin Cities Flying Field, the first airfield in Minneapolis.

"You get to work at the flying field?" Larry's eyes were wide in disbelief.

Greg nodded, smiling. "That's right."

"Wow! That must be the greatest job in the world." Larry thought a moment. "Except for being a pilot or an engineer who works on airplanes."

Greg laughed. "Any other exceptions? I don't want to be a pilot or an engineer, so I think this job is tops."

The beginning of August, Greg came home with news.

"An airmail system is going to be started between Minneapolis and Chicago," he told Larry and Jack. "The first flight will arrive August 10. The barnstormers are going to put on a show at the Twin Cities Flying Field to celebrate when the mail flight arrives. Luke is going to be in the show."

"A show!" Larry was all attention. "That means there will be planes doing aerial acrobatics. Will Luke be doing tricks, too?"

Greg shrugged. "I guess so."

Larry and Jack grinned at each other. They'd only seen Luke fly passengers around on normal flights. They'd never seen him do acrobatic tricks.

Larry could hardly sleep the night before the show. Finally he was going to see Luke again!

CHAPTER 7

Danger in the Air

"I thought this day would never get here!" Larry grabbed hold of a strap in the middle of the crowded trolley car and grinned at Jack.

"It seems like everyone in Minneapolis is going to the flying field," Jack said.

There had been so many people waiting for a trolley car at the corner that they'd had to wait for the fourth one to come along before they could get on. Greg, Larry's family, and Gloria's friend Mabel, were all on the car, too.

Larry grinned, swaying with the motion of the clacking trolley car. "The last time I remember a trolley car being this packed was when we went to see Greg and the rest of the soldiers returning from the war."

The trolley car bell rang. The boys held on tight while the car came to a stop at a street corner. Some of the passengers got off but more got back on.

Jack made a face. "Now I know what a sardine feels like, packed into a little can."

Larry waved a hand in front of his face and wrinkled his nose. He didn't mind the crowd so much, but he wished there weren't so many men smoking cigars on the trolley!

"Father has a friend who lives in Washington, D.C.," Larry told Jack. "He wrote the man a letter and asked him to write back and tell him how long it took for the letter to travel from Minneapolis to his house. Father hopes the letter will travel the whole way by air!"

"Let's see." Jack stared at the ceiling and squinted, trying to figure it out. "Mail has been sent by air between New York City and Washington, and between New York City and Chicago, for a little over a year now. Only takes about ten hours to fly from New York to Chicago." He counted on his fingers. "Wow, your father's letter will probably arrive in Washington in only a couple days."

Larry grinned. "Wish it was me instead of the letter flying to Washington!"

When they finally reached the field, they joined thousands of others to wait for the flight from Chicago. Everyone was excited and laughing and talking, as though it was a circus day. People kept watching the air for the promised plane to appear.

On the field were other planes. Larry pointed them out to Jack. "Those must be the planes that will be putting on the show."

"Greg said the show won't start until after the mail plane arrives," Jack told him. "He says there won't be anything to celebrate if the plane doesn't make it."

Larry thought he recognized Luke's plane, *Josephine,* among the rest. He wished he could talk with Luke, but he couldn't see him.

Father asked, "Did you boys know that the flying field used to be the Twin Cities Motor Speedway? A lot of famous drivers raced here."

Larry nodded.

"Eddie Rickenbacker raced motor cars here, you know," Father said, "before he entered the war."

Jack looked at him in surprise. "Eddie Rickenbacker, the ace pilot?"

Father nodded. "The same."

Gloria frowned. "What is an ace? I know it's a pilot who fought in the Great War, but not every fighting pilot is an ace, is he?"

Larry didn't wait for Father to answer. "To be an ace, an American pilot has to shoot down five planes."

"Oh."

Larry didn't think she looked impressed. "It's not very easy to hit a moving plane in the air while you're trying not to get shot yourself, you know."

She shrugged. "I suppose not."

"Eddie Rickenbacker didn't just shoot down five planes," Jack told her. "He shot twenty-six planes. He shot down more planes than any other American pilot."

"More planes than any pilot in the war?" Gloria asked.

"Well, no," Larry admitted. "A German pilot named Baron von Richthofen shot down the most."

"Eighty!" Jack said, his eyes wide. "The Red Baron shot down eighty Allied planes!"

Gloria's blue eyes widened, too. "My! That *is* a lot!"

Larry looked back at the sky, watching for the mail plane,

satisfied his little sister finally understood what a great thing it was to be an ace.

"Look!" Larry pointed toward the sky. "Is that a plane?"

Everyone around them looked, shading their eyes with their hands or pulling hat brims down so they could see better. A small, dark gray spot seemed to be in the sky a long way off.

A rumble of voices filled with excitement built as more and more people saw the spot. Before long, the dot grew larger.

"It *is* a plane!" Larry cried.

"But is it the mail plane?" Jack asked, still watching the growing dot. "It could be some other plane."

It was the mail plane. It circled the flying field, low enough that Larry and the other people on the ground could see the pilot grin and wave at them.

People began cheering. They waved hats, flags, folded newspapers, and anything else they could get their hands on. A band began playing "America," and soon thousands of people at the field joined in the song.

When the plane landed, people rushed toward it, eager to greet the pilot.

"Whoa! You boys stay here," Father said as Larry and Jack started running toward the plane.

"Aw, shucks!" Larry kicked at a tuft of grass.

"Shucks!" Harry stuck his hands in his knickers and kicked at the ground, too.

A couple policemen escorted the pilot to the wooden platform that had been built for the day's events. If it weren't for the policemen, Larry figured it would have taken hours for the pilot to make it across the field. Everyone wanted to shake his hand.

On the platform, the mayors of Minneapolis and St. Paul shook hands with the pilot and thanked him for flying the first mail plane to the Twin Cities. Then they spoke of how this was the beginning of a new time in America.

It was all interesting, but Larry was glad when the speeches were over, the airmail plane had been taxied over to a hangar, and it was time for the show to begin.

Larry tugged his hat down tighter over his head. Quite a breeze had suddenly come up. He could see it blowing Gloria's short hair about. If it weren't for the red bow that held her hair at the side of her head, her hair would have been blown into her eyes.

He squinted toward the sky. Were those clouds on the horizon? He hoped the wind wouldn't cause trouble for the pilots.

The planes taxied around the field in a row. People cleared back from the field. Slowly the crowd quit talking. Soon the only noise was the engines of the show planes.

ZOOM! ZOOM! ZOOM!

One right after another, the planes followed each other into the air.

Larry forgot the wind as soon as the planes took off.

"They're right on each other's tails!" Larry yelled over the noise of the engines.

Prickles raced over Larry's skin. If one of the engines stalled or a pilot made an unexpected move, all the planes would crash into each other!

The planes raced back and forth over the field, nose to tail. Then over and under each other almost faster than the eye could follow.

The announcer told the crowd that next the pilots would give them an example of a dogfight.

Larry felt someone jerking his sleeve. He looked down, impatient. "What do you want, Harry?"

"Where are the dogs?"

"What dogs?"

"The dogs that are going to fight."

Jack and Father burst into laughter.

Larry smiled. "There aren't any dogs. Dogfights are what battles between planes were called in the Great War." He pointed at the planes. "Just watch, you'll see."

The planes chased each other about the sky. When one came up on the tail of another, the plane in front would bank to one side and slide away. A couple minutes later, the one that had slid away would be on the tail of the other. With every maneuver, the crowd roared their approval.

Larry hardly breathed as he watched. His gaze was glued on the small planes above, but in his mind, he wasn't on the ground watching them. He was imagining himself in one of those planes, fighting a battle over Europe, and coming back to his base afterward, an ace.

Finally all but one of the planes landed.

"And now, for the acrobatics!" The announcer's voice rang out over the flying field.

The plane was climbing higher. The crowd watched, quiet.

Finally, the plane leveled off. Suddenly it started diving toward earth.

The crowd gasped.

Larry's stomach flipped over. Even though he knew the pilot was making the dive on purpose, it still looked like the plane was going to crash nose-first into the ground.

"I can't look!" Gloria put her hands over her face.

Larry glanced at her and then back at the sky. "It's okay. He's flying almost level again. Look!"

From the corner of his eye, he saw her take her hands down just enough to see. "Oh! He's upside down!" Her fingers went back over her eyes.

The plane rolled over until it was right side up again.

"A sideways rollover! Wasn't that great?" Larry asked Jack.

The pilot did a couple more tricks and then landed. When

the plane landed, the crowd groaned their disappointment. They wanted to see more.

No sooner had the plane landed, than another took off.

"It's Luke!" Larry called out.

Josephine climbed high above the field. Luke leveled off the plane. Suddenly, *Josephine* went into a dive, just like the previous plane.

"Oh, not again!" Gloria's hands covered her face once more.

Not taking his gaze from the sky, Larry grabbed one of her wrists. "You have to watch, Gloria. Luke knows what he's doing."

The plane rolled over and leveled off. The crowd gasped.

"He's looping the loop!" Larry called to Gloria and Jack.

A moment later, *Josephine*'s nose was pointed straight up again. Then Luke leveled off the plane and flew it back across the space where *Josephine* had taken her dive.

"You're right," Jack said. "He did make a loop. Wow! That's something to see, all right."

Josephine's nose headed higher.

"Watch this time, Gloria," Larry encouraged. "You don't know when you'll get a chance to see something like this again. This is pretty tricky flying!"

Gloria kept her hands over her face, but Larry saw that she split her fingers so she could watch between them.

Josephine climbed and climbed. For a second, she seemed to hang in the air with her nose pointed toward heaven.

Josephine started sliding toward earth, tail first.

The crowd gasped again. Hundreds of arms pointed toward the sky.

"Oh, he'll get killed!" Gloria cried, closing her fingers over her eyes again.

Larry's heart jumped to his throat, even though he knew

this was part of the trick. "He's not going to get killed. He's doing a backward dive. It's a great trick. Watch!"

He didn't look to see whether she took his advice. He was too busy watching Luke and *Josephine*.

Josephine's tail started to slip slowly from pointing toward the earth to pointing toward the sky. Again, she seemed to stop a moment, hovering in the air. Then she plunged head first toward the earth.

Larry's heart seemed to stop. He grabbed Father's arm. "He shouldn't be going straight down like that! He's supposed to head down at an angle. Something's wrong!"

CHAPTER 8

A Mysterious Pilot

"Come on, Luke! Come on!" Larry whispered, staring in horror at the sky.

But Luke and *Josephine* kept plummeting toward earth.

The crowd realized that something was wrong. People gasped. Children screamed.

Larry prayed, "Help him, God!" His voice was a whisper, but he knew God could hear it. Would He answer?

Terror filled Larry's chest until he thought he would explode. If *Josephine* crashed into the earth, Luke would be sure to die! Lots of barnstormers died doing tricks with their planes, Larry knew. *But not Luke!* he thought.

Josephine's nose turned just a hair.

Larry grabbed his father's arm again. Was Luke pulling *Josephine* out of the dive? Was there time before they smashed into the earth? "Come on, Luke!"

Josephine angled out of the dive, flying straight only five feet above the field.

Larry let out his breath. Luke had done it!

The crowd went wild, cheering and tossing hats in the air.

Jack grabbed Larry's shoulders and shook them. "He did it!"

Larry saw Gloria pull a handkerchief out of her pocket and wipe the tears from her face. Usually he would tease her for crying in public. Not this time. He knew if Luke had crashed, he'd be crying, too.

He put an arm about her shoulders and gave her a quick squeeze. "He's all right. Didn't I tell you he was a good pilot?"

She gave him a shaky smile.

Luke didn't try another trick. Instead, he landed *Josephine* and let another flyer perform.

Larry didn't admit it to the others, but he was glad when the show was over. He hadn't been so frightened since his mother and Harry had come down with the flu two winters ago.

As they left the field, he said to God silently, *I almost forgot! Thank You for helping Luke.*

"Mother, my hands are getting tired," Gloria complained a few days later. "Can you whip the cream?"

She continued to turn the handle of the egg beater, but slowly.

"After I check on the cake," Mother said, hurrying across the kitchen toward the oven. "Is the cream thickening?"

"Yes, but it's not thick enough yet, and I don't think I can turn this much longer."

Heat and a pleasant aroma rolled out into the kitchen when Mother opened the oven door. "Oh, good. I believe it's done. The top is nicely golden and beginning to crack." She took out an angel food cake and turned it upside down over the neck of a bottle in the middle of the kitchen table.

Crash!

Mother jerked upright.

Gloria jumped, almost dropping the beater.

"What are the boys into now?" Mother asked, hurrying through the swinging door into the hallway.

A minute later she was back with Fred in her arms. He was wearing a big grin and holding a large silver spoon.

Mother set him in the middle of the kitchen floor. "Stay there." Taking a kettle from the cupboard, she handed it to him. "Here, pound on this."

Fred did as she said, hitting the bottom of the kettle again and again with the spoon, laughing all the while.

Gloria put her hands to her ears. "Mo-o-ther!"

"I'm sorry, Gloria, but I have to keep him where I can see him. Do you know what he was doing in the parlor? Banging on the brass planter with that spoon."

"Wasn't Larry watching him?"

"No. I told him he had to watch the boys while we prepared for the meeting and during the meeting, too. I don't know where he's off to!"

Fred continued to pound on the kettle.

"Mother, can't we give him something quieter to play with?"

"Fifteen-month-old boys love things that make noise." Mother took the beater from Gloria and started beating the cream. "Will you wash off the blueberries?"

Gloria shook her hands, trying to relax the stiff muscles. "Larry better get back before the meeting."

Mother sighed. "If he isn't back before the League of Women Voters begins its meeting, I'm afraid you're going to have to watch Harry and Fred."

"But, Mother! We're making the final plans for the garden party carnival today!"

"I know you want to help, but someone has to watch the boys. I can't have them disturbing the meeting."

Anger surged through Gloria as she carried a pail of blueberries to the counter beside the sink. "That Larry! He's been sneaking off more and more when he's supposed to be watching the boys, and leaving me to do his work! He's probably off watching those barnstormers again. You know what he told me once? He thinks airplanes are prettier than wedding dresses! Can you imagine?"

Gloria was right. Larry and Jack were right that minute in a field with Luke, watching him check over *Josephine*'s engine. It was the first time they'd seen him since the show, and Larry had what seemed like a million questions.

"Was something wrong with *Josephine*'s engine at the show?" he asked. "Was that why you had trouble?"

"No, nothing like that." Luke grunted as he tightened a screw. "It was the wind. I thought I knew which way the air currents were coming. Then suddenly, a wave of air came at me from a different direction."

"I remember the wind came up right before the show started," Larry said.

"A pilot has to always watch the wind," Luke told the boys, continuing to work on his engine. "If he doesn't judge it right, anything can happen. Like at the show."

"I thought you were a goner," Jack said.

"Can't think like that in an emergency," Luke said, "or you might not do what you need to in order to save yourself. You have to always look for the way out."

"What was your way out?" Larry asked.

"Well, when the blast of air hit me, it about pulled me out of the cockpit. Jerked open my safety belt. My parachute saved me."

"I didn't see your parachute open," Jack said. "How could it? You never jumped out of the plane!"

"The closed chute caught on the cockpit's cowl—the rim on the edge of the cockpit. Still, I had to dig my heels beneath the seat to stay inside the plane."

Prickles inchwormed up Larry's spine. Luke had come closer to dying than he'd been able to tell at the time!

Jack leaned his arms against the bottom wing and stared up at Luke. "Was that the closest call you ever had?"

"Oh, I've had some about as bad during the war."

Larry remembered the conversation they'd had about aces at the flying field. "Are you an ace, Luke?"

"Nope. Only shot down four planes. That was enough. When you're fighting, you know if you don't hit the enemy, they might hit you. Still, it isn't any fun to watch another pilot go down with his plane."

Larry didn't know what to say. He'd always thought of dog-fights as kind of a game—knocking down the enemy's planes, not real live people.

"You know," Luke told them, "when the war started, people had a hard time shooting from an airplane. If they shot over the front of the plane, they'd sometimes shoot their own propellers. Sometimes a scouting plane would fly over the top of the enemy plane and knock the enemy plane out of the air by dumping a load of bricks on him."

Larry and Jack laughed. "You're kidding!" Larry said.

"Nope. It wasn't very sophisticated, but it worked. The Germans first figured out how to time a machine gun so it wouldn't hit the propellers when you shot over the plane's nose, but the Allies caught on quick."

"Did you have a gunner who sat in the other cockpit when you flew?" Jack asked.

"Depended on what I was flying for. When I was flying as a fighter plane, I had a gunner in the other cockpit. When I was on scouting missions, the man who sat in the other cockpit mainly took pictures so we could show our leaders what the other army was doing on the ground, and they could make better battle plans."

"Didn't the other man work the wireless, too, to keep you in touch with the base?" Larry asked.

"Usually. The wireless can be tricky, though. Doesn't always work. Especially if there's a storm or mountains or some other kind of interference. Then, too, sometimes an enemy bullet wiped out the wireless. We often brought homing pigeons with us."

"Pigeons?" Jack asked.

"Yep. Believe it or not, they carried messages back to base. Helped on a lot of missions. Of course, sometimes they got back too late to help. A dog may be man's best friend, but a pigeon is a pilot's best friend."

"What kind of messages did they carry?" Larry asked.

"Well, they'd tell if you spotted enemy ships in the ocean or if you were having trouble with your plane and needed help. Things like that. Near the end of war a pigeon was sent back to base by a British plane out over the Atlantic. They were being shot at by enemy boats and wanted help sent. It was a miracle the pigeon reached the base. It had been shot and died shortly after completing its mission. The base sent help, but it was too late. The enemy must have shot the plane down, and it sunk in the ocean. It was never found. But at least the Allies had a pretty good idea what happened to the plane and the men on board it."

The boys were silent. Larry didn't like to remember all the horrors of the war. He changed the subject.

"I was surprised when Greg told us you'd be out here today selling rides again. I thought you would be off to another city with the show."

"Quit the show." Luke didn't look at them. He kept working on the engine. "Too dangerous."

"Isn't all flying dangerous?" Jack asked.

"Yes, but it's not the same. When you're doing acrobatics, you put your plane into extradangerous positions. You test it and yourself to the limit. That's all right sometimes. If a fighter pilot didn't know how to do acrobatics, he probably wouldn't live very long when he was put into war. When you learn stunts, you put your plane into every possible position and learn how to bring it out safely. When you're in the middle of battle or even in a bad storm, you don't have to take time to think about what to do when your plane is in a strange position. You just do what you learned to do with the stunts."

"Makes sense," Larry said.

Jack shrugged. "So what's the bad part about being in a show?"

Luke pulled his head back from the engine, leaned against the plane, and looked down at them, wrench in hand. "Most of the people who watch barnstormers want to see what pilots can do with airplanes. After all, people have really been flying for less than twenty years. Crowds are fascinated by what men do in the air. Then there are the thrill seekers. They aren't there to see what you can do. They don't care if you live or die."

He paused. Larry and Jack glanced at each other, not speaking.

"Uh, will you show me what you do when you check your engine over like this?" Larry asked.

"Sure. Come on up here."

Larry climbed up beside him.

"It's nothing too difficult. When you fly, the engine vibrates. That can loosen screws and bolts. So I go over it often, checking every screw and nut I can see and trying to tighten them. Most of the time, I can't budge them. That's good. But every once in awhile, I find one that's started to loosen."

He handed Larry the wrench and pointed to a nut and bolt "Here. Check that bolt. See if it's tight."

Larry leaned over the edge of the engine housing and put the end of the wrench around the nut Luke had pointed out. It moved a quarter turn before stopping.

"You see? Good thing we're checking!" Luke encouraged him.

"It wasn't very loose," Larry said.

"Doesn't have to be. If we didn't tighten it now, it would be a lot looser after another day of flying. Might even come off, and that could spell disaster."

A droning sound turned their faces to the sky. A biplane flew low over the field.

"A DH-4," Larry said.

"It sure is." Luke groaned.

Larry looked at him in surprise. "What's the matter? Are you afraid he'll take business away from you?" He'd learned since he'd last seen Luke that often barnstormers wanted a field to themselves so they could make all the money possible from the people who wanted rides.

"No. So close to Minneapolis, there's always enough passengers to go around. This pilot just doesn't happen to be one of my favorites."

Larry glanced over in surprise. He'd never heard Luke say anything against another person before. Why didn't he like this guy? "What's his name?"

"Clyde Bonner."

Bonner's plane banked, circled, and came in for a landing. The pilot jumped out and headed across the field toward them before the propeller stopped whirling.

He stopped beside the wing, pulling off his gloves. "Hi, Luke. Looks like you have yourself a mechanic."

Larry grinned.

Luke didn't. "Sounds like you need one."

Bonner shrugged. "I'll check the engine out later. Got me here without any trouble. I'm sure whatever it is isn't serious."

"Think we're done here, Larry," Luke said. "Thanks for the help."

"Sure thing." Larry slid down, landing beside Bonner. He blinked in surprise. The man smelled kind of funny. A yeasty kind of smell, like when his mother made bread, but harsher.

"We'd better be getting home," Jack said. "It'll be dark soon."

As the two of them walked down the road and into the edge of the city, Larry said, "Did you think Bonner smelled funny?"

"I don't know about funny, but he smelled," Jack answered. "I think he'd been drinking."

Larry stopped short and stared at him. "Drinking? You mean, like liquor?"

Jack nodded.

"But that's not legal! The Prohibition law started last January!"

Suffragists like Larry's mother had fought for Prohibition, which made it against the law to sell and drink alcoholic drinks. Larry's parents had always said that men and women who drank too much often made life hard and unhappy for themselves and their children.

Jack shrugged. "Haven't you heard about bootlegging? You

know, making and selling liquor in secret? The law hasn't stopped everyone from drinking."

A creepy feeling crawled up Larry's spine.

CHAPTER 9

Trouble at the Carnival

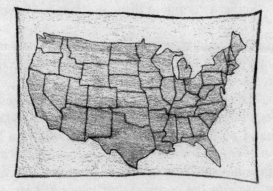

Mother carefully lowered a blueberry pie into a low basket and covered it with a clean blue-checked cloth. "There! That's the last thing, I think. Gloria, did you get all the jellies and pickles we canned?"

"Yes, Mother. They're in a large basket on the front porch, all ready to go." Gloria plopped down on the edge of a kitchen chair.

"And the doughnuts?" Mother asked.

"In this basket on the table." Gloria lifted the red-and-white-striped linen towel from the basket to show her the golden circles.

Larry took advantage of her move to grab one of the doughnuts. "Yum! These look good!"

"Hey! Those are for the garden party!" Gloria slapped at his hand but missed. He was already taking a bite.

"Just testing them for you," he said with his mouth full. "You wouldn't want to sell lousy doughnuts, would you?"

Mother crossed her arms across the front of her purple georgette dress. "I will have you know, Lawrence Allerton, that your sister and I do not make lousy doughnuts!"

Larry swallowed. "You're right. These are great."

"You can carry them out to the motor car for us," Mother told him. "Father is going to drive us since we have so much to carry."

It was going to be a treat, riding in Father's new motor car! They'd only ridden in it a few times. Most of the time, they still walked or rode trolleys.

"Now, Larry," Mother said as he picked up the basket of doughnuts, "I don't want you to shirk your duty today. I don't know when I've been so angry as I was with you last week when you went out to watch the barnstormers instead of watching the boys! There will be none of that today. You and Jack may come to the carnival, but you *will* keep an eye on Harry and Fred."

"Sure, Mother."

"You'd better!" Gloria said. "I had to watch them the other day when you were playing."

"So? I watch them plenty!"

She stamped her foot. "I had to miss the meeting because of you! I don't want to miss the carnival, too."

"You won't." Larry made a face at her.

That only made her angrier. But he was out of the kitchen before she could say anything else.

An hour later, when they were at the carnival in Clara

Ueland's huge yard, Larry was already wishing he had a way to get out of watching Harry and Fred. At least he'd thought to bring the wagon with the wooden plane on top for Fred to ride in.

Even though Larry was there with his mother, he and Jack had to pay fifty cents to attend, the same as other boys and men who came to the carnival. Girls and women only paid twenty-five cents.

"Hey, that's not fair!" Jack protested.

The young woman collecting the money smiled. "Males have more rights than females in America. It's only right they should pay more to enjoy things."

"If the states ratify the Nineteenth Amendment," Larry asked, "will you charge women fifty cents to get in to the carnival next year?"

Her smile had grown wider. "We'll see."

"Let's see where that music is coming from," Jack said.

They followed the cheerful sound around a large hedge. A band in colorful European costumes was playing. Men and women in equally colorful costumes were doing folk dances. People stood in a large circle about them, clapping in time to the music.

Harry and Fred started clapping, too, though Fred didn't clap in time. He just clapped! His blue eyes sparkled with fun, and the sun glinted off the strawberry-blond hair that was so much like Larry's.

Harry tried to copy the dancers, bouncing up and down and holding his arms over his head.

The people around them laughed and pointed at Harry. One of the dancers saw him and brought him into the middle to dance with the group. Then the dancers invited anyone who wanted to join them to try to learn the steps of the folk dance.

When the man who had brought Harry into the middle

beckoned to Larry, Larry backed away, shaking his head. It looked like fun, but he was afraid he'd make a fool of himself. Jack didn't dance, either.

Eventually the band took a break, and the boys drifted on to another event. Harry's face was red from his dancing, and his dark eyes were bright with delight. "What's next, Larry?"

"There's supposed to be a girls' track meet. Want to see that?"

"Sure!" Harry was always ready to try anything.

Jack grinned over Harry's head at Larry. "This should be good. Girls doing track events!"

"I've seen them at the carnival in other years. You'll be surprised. Some of the girls are really good. Gloria and Mabel wanted to be in it this year but decided not to because the older girls are so much better than they are."

The girls were competing in broad jump when the boys found the track meet. Girls seldom wore anything but dresses. It seemed funny to see them wearing wide short pants. One of the girls jumping was Brenda Ueland, Clara Ueland's daughter.

Larry pointed her out to Jack. "Watch her, she's good."

After the broad jump, there was a short speech, telling of the work the League of Women Voters was doing to educate the new women voters of Minnesota. Then there was a pole vaulting contest. Larry liked that best of all. They moved on when Fred started fussing.

"I guess he thinks pole vaulting is boring," Larry told Jack with a grin. "Probably because he can barely walk, let alone pole vault!"

They watched some girls in a tennis match for a while, then moved on again, stopping when they heard another band.

"That sounds like strange music," Jack said.

When they found the musicians, they laughed. "It's a dish-pan band," Larry said. They had fun stomping and clapping in time with the beat of the overturned tin dishpans.

"I'm thirsty," Harry complained when the band finished their tune.

"There's a lemonade stand over by the lilac bushes," Larry said. "But let's stop in at the country store first and see if we can find something to snack on with our lemonade."

The country store was beneath a large red-and-white canopy. Slabs of wood laid across sawhorses made up tables on which the goods for sale were displayed. The boys passed by quilts, knit booties, sweaters, baby bonnets, lace-edged handkerchiefs, and thick potholders before they came to the food.

Pies and cakes of every description made Larry's mouth water, but they were too large for a snack. Baskets of shiny apples and green, yellow, and orange vegetables didn't look appealing.

"Mother and Gloria canned some of those," he told Jack, pointing at glass jars filled with colorful jellies.

"Maybe we should have a chicken!" Harry chuckled and pointed at some white chickens cackling about in a large wooden cage at the edge of the booth.

"Hey, there are the doughnuts!" Larry spotted trays of golden doughnuts like those he'd carried in for his mother. At the table, women were also selling cookies, slices of pie, pieces of cake, and coffee.

Larry bought a doughnut for himself and one for Fred. Jack and Harry wanted sugar cookies. Then they went outside, bought tall, cold glasses of homemade lemonade, and rested in the shade of the tall lilac bushes beside the stand.

"What's that?" Harry asked, pointing to a distant part of the lawn where kids were hopping about, sometimes on two feet, sometimes on one.

"Let's find out," Larry said. They returned their empty

glasses to the lemonade stand and wandered over to where, as he said to Harry, "People look like hopping flamingoes."

A huge map of the forty-eight states had been painted in white on the grass. A red-haired boy was jumping from one state to another. Larry recognized him as Ronald from Gloria's class.

"Wrong!" A young woman in a white dress called out as he jumped onto Tennessee with both feet.

"Aw, shoot!" Ronald stopped jumping and stalked away.

"What's the game?" Larry asked the young woman.

"Hoppetaria. You hop on both feet from one state that's ratified the Nineteenth Amendment to another. In states that have their own laws allowing women to vote but haven't yet ratified the Nineteenth Amendment, you hop on one foot. If you hop on a state that neither has its own laws allowing women to vote nor passed the Nineteenth Amendment, you lose."

Larry grinned. "That doesn't sound so hard. What's the prize?"

"Your choice of the books on that bench." She waved toward a park-style bench nearby, piled with books. "But not too many people have won so far today."

"No wonder Ronald lost," Larry told Jack. "Tennessee is talking about voting on whether or not to ratify the amendment this month. If it does, it will be the thirty-sixth state to ratify it, and it will finally be law in every state—even the ones that voted against it."

Larry went over to the bench and checked out the books. "Hey, look, Jack, here's a Tom Swift book! And one of the new Edward Spring books about fighter aces in the Great War! Boy, I'd sure like both of them."

"Maybe you should try the game," Jack suggested. "It should be a cinch for you with all the talk about women's suffrage you hear from Gloria and your mother."

"Why don't you play, too? Then we could get both books and share them."

"Well, I'm not so sure, but I'll try."

"I want to try, too," Harry said.

Larry shook his head. "It would only be a waste of money. You don't know which states haven't voted for the amendment."

Harry plopped down on the ground, his mouth turned down in a pout.

Jack dug in the pocket of his trousers for a nickel and handed it to the young woman. While jumping about the map, he concentrated hard. "Don't want to slip and step on a state by mistake," he told Larry.

Jack covered half the country without making a mistake. Then he jumped on Maryland.

Larry threw up his hands. "Jack! Maryland hasn't ratified the amendment!"

Jack put down both feet and stared at him. "I thought only the southeastern states hadn't. Maryland isn't in the south."

"Almost."

"Your friend is right," said the girl in charge. "You did a good job, though. Better than most boys and men."

"Thanks," Jack said as he walked off the map. "But that won't win me a book."

Larry paid his nickel and started jumping, remembering to use only one foot in Minnesota. He was almost done when he heard his mother's voice asking Harry what he was doing. In a hurry, he finished.

"Great!" The girl gave him a big grin. "You must really keep up with the news."

Larry nodded at his mother. "She's the one who doesn't let me forget what's happening with the suffrage laws."

The girl laughed. "Good for her. Choose a book for yourself."

Mother was clapping her hands, her eyes sparkling. "You

won, Larry! I'm so proud of you!"

"He jumped like a flamingo in Minnesota," Harry told Mother, looking very important.

Larry had a hard time deciding between the books but finally chose the novel about the fighter pilots.

"I'm going to help with the Hoppetaria game for a while," Mother said. "Have you boys been to the White Elephant yet?"

Larry shook his head.

Harry jumped to his feet. "There's an elephant here? Where? Can we ride him? I always wanted to ride an elephant!"

Mother laughed. "There's no elephant."

Harry's shoulders drooped. "Oh. I wanted to see an elephant."

Mother explained. "A White Elephant booth is where you put a fishing pole over the top of the booth and get a surprise on the end of it. That's where Gloria and Mabel are working."

Fred cried when they started to leave Mother to go to Gloria's booth. "Muvver!" He held his hands out to her, wailing.

"Can we leave him here with you?" Larry asked her hopefully.

Mother shook her head. "If I have to watch him, I won't be able to do my work."

With a groan, Larry picked up the crying Fred. "You pull the wagon," he told Harry. "Maybe Fred will stop crying if I hold him."

Fred was still sobbing when they reached Gloria's booth. Mabel was outside the booth, collecting money. Gloria was behind a striped tentlike structure with four walls and no roof. Mabel stuck her head through some folds of fabric in the wall and told her that her brothers were there.

"Freddie, what's the matter?" Gloria held out her arms to him. He went to her right away. In only a couple minutes, his sobs turned to sniffles and then went away.

"Do you want to fish for a White Elephant?" Gloria asked Harry.

"Yes!"

Larry told her what Harry had said when he first heard of the White Elephant booth. She laughed. "I know just the thing for him."

She set Fred down on the grass and turned to go into her booth, but Fred let out a wail. With a sigh, she took his hand and brought him into the booth with her.

Mabel showed Harry how to put the bamboo fishing pole against the side of the booth so the string hung inside, where Gloria was. "When you feel a tug, pull it back," she told him.

Harry's eyes were wide while he waited for the tug. When it finally came, he backed up, bringing the fishing pole and line with him. A surprise was tied to the end of the line.

"It's an elephant! A real elephant!" he cried in delight.

It was an elephant, carved of wood. Larry thought it was an ugly thing, but at least Harry was happy with it. He untied it for him, and Harry clutched it close.

"How did Glory get a elephant in there?" he asked Mabel.

"Glory has piles and piles of things in there," she answered. "Look for yourself." She showed him where the folds of the tent opened, and he hurried inside.

"You wouldn't believe some of the things in there," Mabel told Jack and Larry. "The women brought lots of old ugly things they didn't want in their houses but didn't think they could give away or sell. That's why it's called a White Elephant booth."

A mother with twin blond girls about five years old stopped to pay Mabel, and Mabel showed them how to use the fishing pole.

Larry nudged Jack and whispered, "Let's get out of here before Harry and Fred come back out of the booth. It won't hurt Gloria to watch them while she works."

While Mabel's back was turned, they hurried away toward the tennis courts.

They'd almost reached them when they heard a loud commotion. Girls and children were screaming! It was coming from the area they'd just left.

Larry and Jack whirled around. "Oh, no!" Larry cried.

The striped booth had fallen. Beneath the bright material were mounds—moving mounds!

CHAPTER 10

In Trouble

Larry and Jack rushed across the lawn toward the fallen booth, dodging other carnival-goers. By the time they reached it, Mabel was helping one of the little girls crawl from beneath what used to be the side of the tent. The girl's mother was helping up the other twin. Both girls were screaming in fright.

So were Harry and Fred.

Larry could hear them but not see them. He could see where they were, though, from punches that came from underneath the pile of material.

"Get us out of here!" Gloria's angry yell was louder than any of the crying.

"We're trying!" Larry called back. "Come on, Jack. Let's get this thing off them."

"Get us out, Larry!" Harry called between sobs. "It's dark!"

"Don't be afraid," he heard Gloria tell him. "It's like a game. Larry will have us out in the sunshine in a minute."

It took more than a minute, but eventually Larry, Jack, and Mabel were able to get them out.

Larry took Fred from Gloria when they were finally free. Fred was still crying. Over his head, Larry asked Gloria, "What happened?"

Gloria's blue eyes flashed with anger. "That's what I'd like to know. Where were you, anyway? Why did you leave Harry and Fred with me? You knew I was working, and you didn't even ask. You just left them!"

Embarrassed, Larry glanced at the crowd that was gathering. Did she have to talk so loud? He kept his voice low, hoping she'd do the same. "I'd been watching them all afternoon. I didn't think it would hurt for you to watch them for a few minutes."

"Not hurt?" Gloria glared at him. "Fred started chewing on the prizes. I got him to stop that. Then when I tied a prize on the end of a fishing pole, Harry tried to help. I got him to stop, but Fred was chewing on something again. I took it away from him, and then I saw Harry was tying something on the fishing pole, but it wasn't what I wanted to give the girl who was fishing. While I was changing it, Fred grabbed the wall to pull himself up. Before I could reach him, he'd pulled the tent down on all of us! And you thought it wouldn't hurt if you didn't do what you were supposed to do! When are you going to stop being so lazy?"

Larry's face burned. He shouldn't have left the boys without telling Gloria. But she didn't have to embarrass him this way! After all, he had helped get the tent off them, hadn't he?

He shoved Fred into her arms. "Here. Hold him while Jack and I fix the tent."

It didn't soothe Gloria's feelings any when he and Jack set

the tent back up and then took Harry and Fred. When they reached home that night, Gloria told Mother and Father the whole story.

Harry added, "It was really, really scary! It was dark, and we couldn't find our way out!"

Larry rolled his eyes and thought, *Thanks a lot, little brother.*

They were in the parlor, resting their feet after the long day and drinking fresh lemonade. Larry could hear moths bumping against the screens on the open windows, and he wished he were outside with them!

Gloria stood in the middle of the room. She stamped her foot. "Larry keeps pushing his work off on me! I watch the boys when I'm supposed to, but lately he keeps dodging out when he's supposed to watch them. Then I have to do his work, too! It's not fair!"

"That's enough, Gloria," Mother said in a mild scolding tone. "Sit down. Father and I will take care of this now."

"But—"

"Sit down, Gloria."

She plopped into an overstuffed dark-blue velvet chair and glared across the room at Larry.

He wanted to stick his tongue out at her, but he knew better with Mother and Father there.

Father leaned forward, his elbows on his knees, his eyes serious. "Gloria is right, Son. It isn't fair."

Larry crossed his arms. "Gloria doesn't watch the boys nearly as much as I have to. It's the middle of August. Summer is going to be over soon, and then we'll be back at school. I want *some* time to do what I please without Harry and Fred hanging on me."

Harry looked up from the wooden elephant he was trotting across the overstuffed sofa. "I don't hang on you! I just like to play with you."

85

Everyone ignored him.

"When Gloria isn't watching the boys," Mother said, "she's often helping me with work for the League of Women Voters or with household chores."

"That's right!" Gloria agreed, sticking her chin out.

Larry's anger boiled over. "Maybe the antisuffragists are right when they say a woman's place is in the home and not in politics. If you two weren't always doing stuff for the League of Women Voters, I wouldn't always have to be doing Gloria's work!"

Mother gasped.

Gloria's mouth dropped open.

"Lawrence!" Father roared, jumping to his feet.

Larry gulped. The blood seemed to seep from his face. He'd done it now!

Father glared down at him. "Don't you ever let me hear you speak to your mother that way again. Apologize to her!"

Larry swallowed hard. "I'm. . .I'm sorry, Mother."

"Looking out for your brothers isn't just women's work," Father told him. "That's what families do. They look out for each other."

"Yes, sir."

Mother's face looked white, but her voice sounded normal. "Teaching you to be responsible and to look out for your younger brothers isn't being a negligent mother. It's training you to be a responsible adult."

"Yes, Mother." *I don't need to be responsible,* he thought. *I'm a kid, not an adult! Summer vacations from school are meant for kids to have fun.*

"Mother is right," Father told him. "Because of your slacking, you won't be allowed to leave the house or yard for a week, unless you are running errands for your mother or going to church."

Larry straightened in his chair. "A week? You can't mean it! Summer is almost over!"

"If it weren't," his father said sharply, "I'd make it two weeks. Maybe after this you won't shirk your duties."

It was the longest week Larry could remember. Every day seemed to last forever. Mother and Father wouldn't even let Jack come over. Larry couldn't get away from Harry and Fred at all.

He read the book he'd won at Hoppetaria all the way through, then read it again. It just made him want to be around airplanes more than ever.

Uncle Erik had done an article for the Minneapolis *Tribune* on the barnstormers. Larry had cut out the article and pictures from the newspaper and pinned them on the wall above his bed. Now when he sat on the bed, reading about the pilots in the war, he looked at the pictures of Luke and the other pilots and daydreamed of being one of them.

When he heard a plane drone over the house, he ran out into the yard, watching it until he couldn't see it anymore. He missed being with the barnstormers more than anything else. What if Luke left Minneapolis before his week was up?

That night, Larry couldn't sleep for worrying about whether Luke had left. When his parents had gone to bed and he could hear Harry's even breathing telling him his brother was asleep, he climbed out of bed.

Quietly he changed into his trousers, a shirt, and a sweater in the light of the moon coming in the bedroom window. Picking up his shoes, he opened the door to the hall and listened. Were Mother and Father asleep? He hoped so!

Holding his breath until his chest hurt, he tiptoed down the hall and down the stairway. He went out the back door, which didn't close as loudly as the front door. Sitting down on the wooden steps, he put on his shoes and laced them up, his heart thumping wildly.

He started across the yard toward the alley. The neighbor's dog saw him and started barking up a storm. He stopped in the shadow of the large oak tree, his back hard against the trunk, listening above the sound of the dog and evening insects. Would the dog wake his parents? Would they look out their bedroom window to see what was making it bark?

No one came to the window. He darted to the shed beside the alley and took out his bike. He couldn't be taking trolleys this time of night, and it was a long way out to the field where he'd last seen Luke.

CHAPTER 11
Midnight Adventures

Moonlight reflected off the wings of two biplanes when Larry reached the field. Was one of them Luke's? He couldn't tell in the dark.

He leaned his bike against the wooden fence and climbed over the fence into the field. He headed straight toward the plane that looked most like Luke's. If it was another pilot's plane, he probably wouldn't welcome a stranger coming on him and his plane in the middle of the night! Pilots were pretty protective of their planes.

"Who's there?" Luke's voice sounded sharp as a pistol shot in the night air.

Larry stopped short. "It's only me, Larry."

"What are you doing out here this time of night? Come on over here and sit down."

When Larry crawled under the wing, Luke was out of his bedroll and seated cross-legged on top of it. "Sit down." He patted the bedroll beside him.

Larry sat down. Mosquitoes were buzzing around. He couldn't see them, but he could hear them. He was glad he'd put on his sweater and hat.

He told Luke about being grounded.

Luke chuckled. "You shouldn't have left your brothers with Gloria, but the tent moving about like boiling gelatin is a pretty funny picture!"

Larry told him why he'd come out to the field so late.

"You needn't have worried. I'm sticking around here for a while." Luke paused. "It's good to see you, but won't you get in trouble for being out at night?"

"If my parents find out, I'll probably be grounded for the rest of my life."

Luke laughed. "I remember making my parents that mad a few times when I was young. I thought I knew what I was doing then. Now I think my parents were probably right when they laid down the rules I broke."

Larry plucked a piece of straw from beside the blanket and broke it in two. He didn't think he'd ever feel his parents were right to expect him to watch his brothers so much!

"Since I got back from the war," Luke said, "I've met a lot of kids, both boys and girls, who are fascinated by flying. But I don't think I've ever met one who loves it as much as you do."

"It's all I think about."

"If you want to be a pilot, there's a lot to learn. You have to understand the engine and know how to take care of your plane. You have to learn what all the instruments are for and how to use the rudder and throttle. You have to learn how to taxi, how to fly straight, how to turn, how to glide, how to take off, how to climb, how to land, how to do spirals, and stalls, and spins."

"Sounds like fun!" Larry plucked another piece of hay and chewed on one end. "When you were a kid, did you want to fly more than anything?"

Luke drew up his legs and slipped his arms about his knees. "Guess I did. When the Wright brothers first proved they could build a plane that could fly, it was 1903, and I was five years old. Flying pretty much took the world by storm. People all over the world wanted to build flying machines, and there were flying races in Europe and America. Pilots learned how to do aerial acrobats and put on shows. People wrote songs about flying."

Larry grinned. "Like 'Come, Josephine, in My Flying Machine'?"

"Yes. Planes made news all the time. In spite of all the newspaper articles telling what was happening, my father didn't believe machines could fly until he saw one fly for himself. A lot of people were like that. Some people said it was a sin to fly, that if God wanted people to fly, He would have given us wings. To me, it seemed a wonderful thing to fly. When I was fifteen, I begged a pilot to take me for a ride. He did, and I was hooked."

"I guess I'm hooked, too," Larry said.

"Yes, I think you are. But from different things you've said, I think you want to be more than just a pilot."

"Yes. I want to fly, but I want to design airplanes, too."

"Why?" Luke asked.

He sounded like he really wanted to know why Larry was

interested in designing planes. So Larry tried to put his feelings into words.

"Remember the men who flew over the Atlantic Ocean this year?"

"Yes."

"Well, I think it's terrific that they did that, but they only flew over the shortest piece of the ocean, between Ireland and Newfoundland."

"That's a long way, over nineteen hundred miles!" Luke reminded him. "A plane can't carry enough fuel to fly much farther than that. A lot of planes can't carry even that much fuel. My *Josephine* can't fly that far in one trip."

"I know. But people are already talking about trying to fly across the widest part of the Atlantic some day. People are trying to build planes that can fly that far. That's what I'd like to do. Build planes that are stronger and fly farther."

"That's a good goal."

Luke's approval made Larry warm to his subject even more. "And remember the plane that flew over Paris last year with twenty-five people aboard? Twenty-five! Imagine if there were lots of planes that could carry that many people, and they were large enough to carry lots of fuel, so they could fly a long way. Think of all the people that could fly at one time! And they could visit any place in the world!"

Luke chuckled. "Sounds like you've got the fever, all right."

"You. . .you don't think I'm being silly?"

"Silly? Of course not!"

"Jack thinks I'm loony. I haven't told anyone but you and Jack what I really want to do."

"You're not loony. Dreamers often see things in their minds that other people can't see until the dreamers make them real. Lots of people tried to build flying machines before the Wright brothers. Even the Wright brothers tried a lot of machines that didn't work so well until Kitty Hawk. Most of the people gave up when their attempts didn't work and people laughed at them. The Wright brothers didn't give up no matter how much people laughed. Thanks to them, I can fly *Josephine*."

"And I've gotten to fly in *Josephine*." Larry grinned.

"Yes. I don't think dreams are silly at all. I think God puts dreams in our hearts to show us what He wants us to do with our lives."

Could that be true? Larry wondered. *It would be wonderful if God meant for me to spend my life working with airplanes!*

"Of course," Luke continued, "that doesn't mean the dreams come easy. Look how long and hard the Wright brothers worked on planes before Kitty Hawk. In 1903, only a couple people knew how to fly a plane. Now, just seventeen years later, it's estimated more than two thousand people around the world know how to fly! But more than two hundred pilots have been killed, and lots of them weren't killed in the war. Dreams can cost a lot."

"I guess they can," Larry said slowly.

Luke bopped him lightly in the shoulder with a fist. "Maybe one day I can be a test pilot for some of the planes you design."

Larry grinned. "Sure thing!" Warmth filled his chest. It was good to know that Luke truly believed in him.

"Hey!" A voice came from the other plane. "Can't a guy get any quiet in the middle of a field? Why don't you two quit talkin' and let a fellow sleep?"

"That's Clyde Bonner," Luke said in a whisper.

"Did he find out what was wrong with his engine the other day?" Larry whispered back.

"I don't think he's checked. I haven't seen him looking his

engine over. He's taken up a few passengers, and I've wondered every time whether his plane was going to crash. The engine still sounds bad." Luke sounded worried.

A shiver ran along Larry's nerves. He didn't like the idea of a pilot taking up passengers in a plane that might not be safe. "Why doesn't he take better care of his plane?"

"Some people aren't too responsible," Luke answered. "A responsible pilot always inspects the plane and engine before flying. There are other things he checks, too. Like the direction of the wind. He sets the altimeter. He makes sure his helmet and goggles are properly adjusted, and—this is very important—he makes sure he has a cloth handy to wipe off his goggles in case of bad weather, and that the cloth isn't in a place from which it can be blown away.

"The engine should be given a ground test," Luke continued, "and the gas valve properly set. If it's a cold time of year or you're flying up high where the air is cold, you have to be careful with your scarf and coat. A coat that's too long can catch in the wind. So can a scarf. Long scarves have caught in propellers and choked the pilots wearing them. And of course the safety belt should be buckled."

Larry shivered, remembering what almost happened to Luke when his safety belt was torn loose. "There's a lot to remember, isn't there?"

"Yes. And every rule is an important one. Flying is fun, but one mistake can cost a pilot his life and the life of his passenger. That's why it bothers me so much that Clyde isn't more responsible."

That worried tone was back in Luke's voice. Larry squirmed a bit at the way he kept talking about responsibility. It reminded him of his parents telling him that he wasn't acting responsibly. Of course, not wanting to watch his little brothers wasn't like not taking care of an airplane. Was it?

Dawn was coloring the sky when Larry slid his bike back in the shed and stole up the stairs to his room. He was careful to avoid the stairs and hall boards he knew creaked. Still, it was a long, slow walk between the back door and his bed. He didn't breathe a sigh of relief until he was in bed and under the covers.

His last thought was that his bed was a lot more comfortable than a bedroll on a hard bumpy field!

CHAPTER 12

The Decision

The next morning, Larry didn't want to get out of bed when his mother called to him for breakfast, but he didn't dare sleep in. His parents might wonder why he was so tired.

Being tired made him grumpy. Or maybe it was feeling guilty about sneaking out the night before that made him grumpy. He wasn't sorry that he'd had that talk with Luke, though.

Mother, who was usually cheerful, was a bit grumpy to-day, too, but not at the family. She was mad at the Tennessee legislators.

"I can't imagine what is taking them so long to decide

whether or not to ratify the amendment." She set a plate of hot-cakes down on the table so hard that Larry jumped.

"So what if they don't?" Larry asked. "You only need one more state to ratify it. There are other states that haven't voted yet."

"Only four besides Tennessee! Thirty-five states have rat-ified it, and eight have voted against it."

"Maybe one of the other four states will vote for it," Larry said.

"You don't understand." Mother set a pitcher of warm maple syrup down beside him. "Tennessee's governor called a special session for the legislators to vote on the amendment. The other four states' governors have refused to call special sessions because they don't want to spend the extra money. So if Tennessee doesn't ratify the amendment, it won't become a fed-eral law until after the 1920 election, if it becomes law at all."

Larry knew why Mother wanted it to become a law so soon. In addition to voting for congressmen and local leaders, people would be voting for the new president of the United States in 1920. Mother wanted all the women in the country to be able to vote for the president. It would be four more years before another presidential election.

"I ran into the head of the Minneapolis Anti-Suffrage League yesterday, and he was positively gloating." Mother brushed her hands against her apron. "He says there isn't a chance the amendment will be ratified, what with almost all the southeastern states voting against it. And Tennessee is a southern state, as he delighted in reminding me."

"Think how happy you'll be when he's proven wrong," Larry suggested. He hoped the man was wrong. His mother would be very unhappy if the amendment wasn't ratified.

"Honestly!" Mother sat down and helped herself to some hotcakes. "I don't understand how the legislators in those states that voted against the amendment can live with themselves. Or with their wives! What must their wives and daughters and mothers think of such men, if the men have so little faith in them?"

"I don't know, Mother." Larry looked at her and started chuckling. He'd hardly ever seen his mother so flustered.

A couple days later, Mother was radiant. Tennessee had ratified the amendment! Now they only had to wait for the federal officials in Washington to verify that enough states had ratified the amendment, and it would become law.

She made a huge cake and invited Grandma Allerton and Uncle Erik's family and Cousin Lydia and her new husband, Donald, to dinner to celebrate.

On August 26, 1920, the Nineteenth Amendment became law. No one could tell women they couldn't vote just because they weren't men.

Reading a newspaper article about the new law to the family that evening, Mother laughed. "Listen to this! It says, 'Congress will be full of beautiful women before twenty-five years have passed, and there will be a woman president.' "

"I hope that's true," Gloria said. "Maybe I can be in Congress!"

Larry rolled his eyes and groaned. Then he remembered what Luke said about dreams, and he wondered.

"I have a surprise for you children." Mother leaned forward in her rocker, her eyes shining. "Tomorrow, the first election in the country that women will vote in under the new amendment is being held in St. Paul."

"Why?" Larry asked. "The election for president and congressmen isn't until November."

"This is just a little election, really. It's only a vote on whether or not St. Paul should sell bonds to pay for improving their water system."

"That doesn't sound like much!" Larry said.

"You'd think so if you were a woman. Remember, most women in the country have never been allowed to vote before," Mother reminded.

"What's the surprise?" Harry asked.

"We're all going to St. Paul in the morning to see the women vote!"

They arose early the next day. Because it was such a special day for Mother, Father took the day off work at the hospital and drove the family to St. Paul in the new car. Larry was glad for his mother that the amendment had been ratified, but he was more excited to ride so far in the car than he was to see women voting.

When they arrived, Larry was surprised to see that they weren't the only people who came to watch the women vote. There were women from Minneapolis carrying banners that said, *We Won the Vote!* The crowd was singing the "Battle Hymn of the Republic."

Uncle Erik saw them and made his way through the crowd to say hello.

"Are you going to do a story on the women voting?" Mother asked.

"I sure am! Exciting, isn't it?"

Mother's smile was huge. "It's wonderful!"

"I'm not the only reporter here. There are reporters from lots of papers." He pointed with a pencil toward a group of men on the other side of the street. "See those men? They're from a California film studio!"

Larry stared at the men. "Are they going to do a film about these ladies?"

"They're filming a newsreel," Uncle Erik said. "These St. Paul women will be shown across the country in newsreels at the flickers!"

Larry looked with new respect at the women lined up in front of the building, waiting their turn to vote. They looked dressed up and were wearing smiles as big as Mother's.

When Larry had a chance, he slipped away from his family and made his way through the crowd to where the film crew was shooting. Their camera was on a tripod. One of the men was looking through it and turning a crank. When one of the crew told the crowd to move, they did as he said.

Larry was disappointed when the crew packed up and left. He made his way back to his family. "Say, aren't we going to take a break and eat today?" he asked. "It's almost noon."

As they went down the street looking for a cafe, Larry teased his mother. "If you don't stop smiling soon, your face will break!"

Mother just laughed. "Oh, Larry. This is a wonderful day for women!"

The next morning, Larry looked for Uncle Erik's article in the paper. It was on the front page, along with a picture of some of the women who had voted.

"Eighty-six women voted yesterday," he read to the family over the breakfast table. "It says here that the women's ballots were specially marked. That way, if someone decides the amendment didn't actually become law in time for them to vote, their votes can be thrown out."

"What a terrible thought!" Mother looked horrified at the possibility.

A headline beneath the picture caught Larry's attention. "City Wet. Federal Agents in Despair." Larry knew *wet* meant people had been found breaking the law by selling or drinking liquor in Minneapolis. The federal agents were upset because they couldn't find the bootleggers who were selling the illegal liquor.

His stomach tightened. The article reminded him of Clyde

Bonner, the barnstormer, and the way he had smelled the day he met him. From what Luke had told him, it sounded like Bonner wasn't taking very good care of his plane, and that was dangerous. Larry knew it was dangerous for a pilot to fly when he'd been drinking liquor, too, even if drinking hadn't been against the law.

Goose bumps ran along his arms as he imagined what could happen if Clyde Bonner was drinking. He sure hoped he was wrong about that man.

CHAPTER 13
Caught!

A few days later, Larry plopped down in a leather-seated rocking chair in the parlor and groaned. "Back to school tomorrow! How could summer have gone by so fast? It seems like it just started."

Mother looked up from the overstuffed chair where she was mending the heel in one of Larry's socks. "I'm going back to school, too."

Larry stared at her in disbelief. She looked as excited as if she'd won the right to vote all over again. "You're teasing, right?"

"No."

"You aren't going to be going to my school, are you?" he

asked slowly. He liked his mother, but he didn't want to meet her in the halls or share a class with her.

"Oh, no. I'm going to the University of Minnesota. They're offering a special five-day course called 'Citizenship for Women Voters.' "

Larry laughed. "I didn't think anyone knew more about being a citizen than you. Maybe you should teach the class."

Mother rested her mending in her lap. "Why, Larry! What a nice thing to say."

Larry squirmed a little, embarrassed. "When do you start?"

"Next week."

"Why are you taking this class?"

"Women in Minnesota have only been able to vote on education and library issues in the past. There's a lot we need to learn in order to make wise decisions when we vote."

"That's what you said the League of Women Voters is all about—to teach women to be wise voters."

"Yes. I guess the university agrees with us."

Every night the following week, Mother came home flushed with excitement. Their evening meals became mini-classes where she told them about the topics that had been discussed.

"We learned how city government works today," she said one night.

"There was a speech about honesty and ideals in politics today," she reported another night. "It was most interesting!"

Then she would go on to repeat as much as she could remember about what had been said.

"I feel like we're taking the class, too," Larry told Jack on their way to school one morning.

Mother learned about the Minnesota Constitution, the hopes and problems of helping immigrants become "Americanized," important topics the state legislators would be voting on in the next session, public health, the problem of millions of people in the country who didn't know how to read, parliamentary practice, how the federal and state governments work, how the government tried to help poor people, freedom of speech, the way the United States tried to help other countries, and the way the United States used food to try to convince other countries to do things certain ways.

"That's very important just now, you know," Mother said, passing the platter of roast beef. "With so many European countries still struggling to put themselves back together after the Great War, they need food. So they are more apt to do as the United States thinks they should if the United States won't give them food for their people unless they do."

Larry shook his head. "How can you learn so much in one week? I can't imagine anyone going to school if they don't have to."

"It's fun!" Mother said, giving him a surprised look.

Larry grunted.

Father smiled at Mother. "Well, I am impressed. You've learned a lot from this course."

"Do you know that more than one thousand women are taking the classes? Our work has paid off, I think. We've convinced women they need to learn to be wise voters."

"I think the classes should be offered to men, too," Father said. "I don't know many men who know as much as you do about the topics taught in those classes."

"Erik agrees with you," Mother said. "He was at the university today so he could write an article for the newspaper about the course."

Uncle Erik wasn't the only newspaperman who agreed with Father. Other reporters and editors wrote about the courses. Soon the classes were offered again to both men and women. Father went to the evening classes when his work at the hospital was over for the day.

Larry still couldn't imagine going to school if you didn't have to! This was the worst year of school Larry could remember. He was bored by the classes.

"What will I ever use all this stuff for, anyway?" he asked his mother one night as he struggled with an especially hard arithmetic problem.

He couldn't seem to concentrate on what his teachers were saying. He was always daydreaming about airplanes or drawing pictures of them instead of listening or learning his lessons.

At home, he ignored his homework whenever he could get away with it. Instead, he spent his evenings and weekends reading books about airplanes or fighter aces. When he wasn't reading about planes and flying, he was building toy-sized planes.

He and Jack still watched the barnstormers whenever they got the chance, but with school, it wasn't as easy. It took time to get to the edge of the city where the barnstormers took people up for rides.

One day, Larry brought the model he'd made of *Josephine* out to show Luke. He was trembling inside when he handed it to the pilot. Would Luke like it? He'd worked so hard to make it as much like the real *Josephine* as possible!

"Why, this is great!" Luke turned the small plane about, examining every detail. "It looks just like her. You used real canvas and carved a wooden propeller and have wooden struts to hold the wings apart. This is just great!" he repeated.

Larry drew a sigh of relief. "It took quite awhile, but I wanted it to be just right."

"I'll say you did it right. You have a plane designer's eye, all right." Luke pointed to the nose. "You even painted *Josephine*'s name on it!"

Pride swept through Larry. He was glad Luke could tell how much work he'd put into it.

After that day, Larry started slipping away from school whenever he could to visit the barnstormers.

He didn't see Luke anymore. Luke had left the area for a while. "I want to visit some other places up north before winter sets in," he told Larry the day before he left. "Think I'll check out some other towns in Minnesota. Maybe South Dakota, or Wisconsin, or Iowa, too."

Larry had sighed. "Sounds a lot more exciting than school!"

Larry's grades started slipping. He hid the papers from his parents and tried to forget that when it was time for quarterly reports, his parents would find out how poorly he was doing.

One late September day, Larry and Jack stole away from the schoolyard after lunch, when everyone was heading back into classes for the day. They hid among the tall elms at the edge of the yard until it was empty of students. Then, grinning at each other, they took off at a run toward a nearby alley.

"It's safer in the alleys than on the sidewalks or streets," Larry told Jack as they jogged along, their leather, ankle-high shoes pounding in the dirt. "The police and truant officers are less likely to see you."

They couldn't stay in the alleys forever. As they stood with some men on a corner waiting for a trolley car, Larry felt a heavy hand clasp his shoulder.

"Hey!" He twitched his shoulder, trying to break free, and scowled up at the man beside him.

"Playing hooky, are we, boys?"

Larry went stone still. His stomach turned over. A truant officer!

CHAPTER 14

The Crash

Larry wished he could turn invisible when the burly truant officer brought him and Jack back to school that afternoon. The principal gave them a lecture. Then he made them sit in his office without talking for the rest of the day. After school, he handed each of them a paper.

"This is a note for your parents. Either your father or mother must sign it so I know you've shown it to them. You are both suspended from school for the next two days." He handed them each another sheet of paper. "Here is a list of assignments you are to have ready when you return to school."

Walking home, Larry grumbled, "Isn't that just like a principal? He gets mad at us for skipping school and punishes us by having us skip two more days of school!"

"Doesn't make much sense to me," Jack agreed, "but I guess these assignments are going to keep us busy while we're at home."

They walked together silently for a few minutes. Then Jack cleared his throat. "Do you. . .do you s'pose our parents are going to be really mad?"

Larry nodded. "I'm sure they will be."

Larry didn't want to think about it, but he couldn't think of anything else. He wished he could fly away with Luke in *Josephine* and never have to tell his father he'd skipped school.

He didn't have to worry about telling Mother. When he got home, Gloria was in the kitchen, talking a mile a minute to Mother.

"It was awful! The whole school knew. Simply everyone! People kept asking me if I knew my brother was in the principal's office for skipping school. I just wanted to die!"

Larry's gaze met Mother's over Gloria's head. He swallowed hard. He didn't know what to say.

He wasn't sure what Mother was thinking. Instead of looking angry, she seemed a little sad. All she said was, "We'll talk about this tonight when your father gets home, Larry."

When Gloria and Harry and Fred were in bed, Father told Larry to join him and Mother in the parlor.

Larry had been dreading this moment ever since he'd seen that big truant officer looking down at him on the street corner. He'd hardly been able to eat dinner.

His parents sat together on the overstuffed sofa. Larry sat in the wooden rocker with the leather seat. He folded his arms over his chest and stared at his mother and father.

Father was the first to speak. "The note from the principal

says he doesn't think this is the first time you've skipped school. Is he right?"

Larry wanted to lie and say the principal was wrong, but somehow, he couldn't. He nodded his head sharply, once.

"How many other times have you played hooky?" Father asked.

Larry shrugged. "I don't remember."

Mother's mouth dropped. "You've skipped so many times that you can't remember?"

Larry bit his bottom lip.

Father rested his elbows on his knees and ran a hand through his hair. He sighed, and Larry thought he sounded tired. "Why, Larry? Where do you go when you skip school?"

Larry shrugged again. "Wherever I can find barnstormers."

Mother shook her head.

"Don't you know how important it is to attend school?" Father asked.

Larry didn't have any answers that would make his parents happy, even if he lied. "I don't see why I need to go to school anymore. I know everything I need to know about history and reading and writing and arithmetic."

"Are you sure?" Father asked in a calm voice. "What do you plan to do to earn a living?"

Larry held his breath, staring at his father. Did he dare tell him what he wanted to do most in the world? "I want to design airplanes," he blurted out finally.

"Do you think anyone will want to fly in them if they know you didn't bother to get a good education?" Father asked, his voice still calm. "Will they feel safe in your planes?"

Larry thought Father's questions sounded silly. "I'm not learning anything in school that I'll need to know to design planes. I already know how to draw and read and write and do sums."

Mother shook her head again. Larry thought he saw tears glimmering in her eyes.

Father sighed and ran his hand through his hair again. "The more you know about arithmetic and algebra and physics, the better you will be at designing planes."

Larry didn't want to hear it. He didn't say anything. He wished Father would yell at him instead of looking at him in that sad way. He had never seen his father look so disappointed in him before. It only made him feel guiltier.

"Since the school is punishing you," Father said, "I guess we won't. The principal's note says you have a list of assignments that need to be done before you go back to school. See that you do them while you are home the next couple days, and show them to me before you return to school."

"Can I go to bed now?" Larry asked, still angry.

"Yes."

Larry stood so fast the rocker almost hit the wall.

"Larry."

He looked at his father.

"I don't want to ever hear that you've played hooky for so much as an hour." Father's voice didn't sound angry, but it was firm. Larry knew he meant it.

Larry nodded and went into the hall and up the stairs.

The next two days, Larry tried to do his assignments at the kitchen table, where he could spread out his papers and books. Fred kept tugging papers off the table. Sometimes he'd crumple them. Sometimes he'd tear them. Sometimes he'd chew on them.

"Mother, can't you do anything about Fred?" Larry demanded half a dozen times.

Mother laughed when she saw Fred eating one of Larry's papers. "Well, he's only acting his age. Will you watch him while I get dinner?"

"Will *I* watch him? I have schoolwork to do!"

"Yes, well, if you were in school, you wouldn't have to watch Fred while you study, would you?" she asked with a smile.

Things didn't get any better after dinner. Friends of Mother's from the League of Women Voters came over. They spent the afternoon in the kitchen and dining room, preparing posters and making plans for their drive to register women to vote in the November election.

Larry didn't have any choice but to try to do his homework on his bed. Soon Mother appeared with Fred in her arms. "Can you watch him? He's getting in our way."

"How am I going to get my schoolwork done?"

Mother shrugged and smiled. "Maybe you should have asked yourself that before you played hooky. When did you plan to get the schoolwork done that you missed when you skipped classes?"

She didn't wait for an answer.

Larry shut his books. He took one of his small airplanes from his dresser and sat down on the floor beside Fred. "You don't know how lucky you are that you aren't in school, buddy. Here. Let me tell you about airplanes."

Finally! Larry thought when he heard Gloria come in after school. *Someone else to watch Fred!*

Gloria shook her head when he asked for help. "I have to make posters for the voter registration booths."

Larry turned to Harry. "I'll let you play with one of my planes if you watch Fred for me."

"Really?" Harry's face brightened.

Harry always wanted to play with Larry's planes, but Larry usually didn't let his little brother touch them.

For a few minutes, Larry was able to do his homework. Then Fred started screaming. Harry was playing with the plane and not letting Fred touch it.

Larry calmed Fred down and went back to his studies, but the rest of the afternoon went the same way. He'd study a few minutes, then have to do something with Harry and Fred.

The next day was almost as bad. The League of Women Voters people were back, still working on the registration drive.

"What are they doing that's taking so much time?" Larry asked his mother angrily at dinner. "What is the registration drive, anyway?"

"Before people are allowed to vote, they have to register. They have to give their name and address and prove that they are American citizens. Because so many women will be voting this year for the first time, we are making posters and flyers to remind them that they need to register. We're setting up information booths in downtown stores where people can ask questions about registering and about voting. I'm going to work in one of the booths two afternoons a week while Grandma Allerton watches Fred."

"But the election isn't until November."

"It's already the end of September. November will be here before you know it. And we've so much to do! We're making 12,500 posters on national issues so the voters will know what the candidates say they will do if they are elected. And we plan to hand out over one hundred thousand flyers on how to register and vote."

"Sounds like a lot of work."

"Most things that are worthwhile take a good deal of effort. But if you like what you're doing, work is fun."

Maybe, Larry thought, *but schoolwork isn't fun!*

Because he'd skipped so many classes, he couldn't figure out his arithmetic problems, even when he wasn't watching Harry and Fred. The night before he went back to school, he had to ask Father for help. He spent an hour trying to get up the courage. He was sure Father would say, "I told you so."

He didn't. He just sat down on the bed beside Larry and helped him figure it out.

Which only made Larry feel guiltier than ever.

A week later, when Jack and Larry were walking home from school, Jack said, "My brother got a letter from Luke. He's coming back to Minneapolis for a bit before winter settles in. He thought he'd be back today."

Right away Larry forgot that he was supposed to go right home from school since he'd been caught playing hooky. "Let's see if he's at the field he was at before!"

"I don't think we should do that today. He wrote Greg that if he got here in time, he'd stop by the house in the evening. We can see him tonight and ask where he'll be flying while he's here."

Larry was only a little disappointed. It would be good to see Luke again.

They'd only gone a couple blocks when Larry heard a plane in the distance. Both boys stopped and searched the cloudless sky. "There it is!" Larry pointed.

"Do you think it's Luke?"

"Too far away to tell. Look, the pilot's climbing. He must be doing tricks."

The boys watched while the plane went higher and higher. Finally it rolled backward and dove toward the earth.

No matter how many times Larry saw aerial acrobatics, his heart raced when a plane dove toward the earth that way!

The plane dove and dove.

"Level out," Larry said.

The plane kept diving, gaining speed.

"It's going to crash!" Jack yelled.

A moment later, the plane disappeared.

Larry and Jack stared at where they'd last seen the plane.

Gray smoke billowed up into the calm blue sky.

"Did you see a parachute?" Larry asked through a tight throat.

Jack shook his head.

The pilot must have been killed, Larry thought. *No one could live through a crash like that.*

"Do you. . ." Jack gulped. "Do you think it was Luke?"

Terror, hot and horrible, flooded Larry's chest. He took off running in the direction of the smoke. *It can't be Luke! It can't!*

CHAPTER 15

In Trouble Again

By the time they reached the trolley line, Larry's chest hurt from running so hard. He flopped down in a seat, trying not to believe Luke was in that crashed plane.

Larry and Jack weren't the only ones who had seen the crash. People on the trolley were excitedly talking about it.

When the trolley had taken them as close as possible to the area where they thought the plane went down, the boys got off. Within a couple minutes, they were caught up in a crowd of people rushing toward the crash site.

The plane had landed nose first. Smoke poured from it, though firemen were spraying water on it with their huge hoses. Through the smoke, Larry could see the charred tail section sticking up in the air.

"A DH-4." He breathed a huge sigh of relief. "It's a DH-4, Jack. It wasn't Luke. *Josephine* is a Jenny."

Larry's eyes smarted with hot tears. He wanted to cry just because he was so glad it wasn't Luke in the smoldering wreck. He swallowed hard and tried to keep his eyes open wide so the tears wouldn't fall.

Jack grabbed his arm. "There! There's a plane like Luke's."

Sure enough, *Josephine* was sitting in a small field, almost hidden by a grove of cottonwood trees. Larry took off at a run. Jack was on his heels.

They saw Luke before they reached *Josephine*. "Whoa!" the pilot called as they rushed toward him. His soft leather helmet covered his blond hair. His goggles were pushed up on his forehead.

His face looks like. . .like he's seen something terrible, Larry thought. "We saw the plane crash from back near the school. We couldn't tell what kind of plane it was. We thought it might be yours!" The words tumbled out. "I'm so glad it wasn't you!"

"Me, too!" Jack said, his voice cracking.

Luke patted their shoulders. "So am I, buddies."

"Was the pilot k. . .killed?" Jack asked.

Luke nodded.

Larry dashed a tear from his cheek with the back of his hand. "Do you know him?"

Luke swallowed and nodded again. "It was Clyde—Clyde Bonner."

Clyde! Larry stared at the plane. Horror washed over him. He'd never known a pilot who'd been killed.

"He must not have fixed whatever was making that bad noise in his engine, huh?" Larry asked.

116

"I don't know," Luke said. "I haven't seen him since I left here last month."

Jack leaned close and asked in a loud whisper, "Do you think he was drinking bootleg liquor? I thought I smelled it on him once."

Luke shrugged. "Guess we'll never know. Might have been, though. I smelled it on him a few times, too."

Larry was surprised to see Uncle Erik and a newspaper photographer over by the burning plane. He went over to say hello. Uncle Erik asked if he'd seen the crash. Larry told him what he and Jack had seen. Then he introduced him to Luke.

Luke told him what he knew about Clyde Bonner. Then Uncle Erik had to get back to the newspaper and write up the story.

Jack saw someone else he knew and went to talk with him, leaving Luke and Larry alone at the edge of the curious crowd.

"I guess it doesn't matter how safe someone designs a plane," Larry said slowly, his eyes on the still smoldering DH-4. "If the pilot doesn't take care of the plane or drinks, accidents will happen."

"You're right."

Larry's scalp prickled, thinking how awful it must have been for Clyde when he realized he was going to crash. "Do you ever get frightened, Luke? About the risks you take as a pilot, I mean. Sometimes even good pilots who take care of their planes crash."

"That's true. But no one gets through life without taking risks. Different people are willing to take different risks. What seems risky to a doctor, like your father, might not seem risky to me. What seems risky to me might not seem risky to your father. Understand?"

"I think so."

"Clyde Bonner took more risks than he had to take," Luke

reminded him. "He didn't take care of his plane well, and he probably flew after he'd been drinking."

They watched for a few minutes as water continued to pour over the wreckage.

"I'd better get home soon," Larry said. "I'll probably be in trouble with Mother and Father for coming here. I'm already in enough trouble with them."

"Why?"

Larry told Luke how he played hooky to watch barnstormers. "I tried to tell Mother and Father that I don't need school. How is what they teach me at school going to help me design planes? What I need to do is learn all I can about planes, don't you think?"

Luke pulled off his goggles and helmet. His blond brows met in a frown. "Yes, I think you need to learn all you can about planes. But I think you need to stay in school and learn what they teach you there, too. There's a lot you have to know if you want to design planes. You have to be good at arithmetic and physics. You have to be able to read and know how to do research. Right now, the most important thing you can do with your time is learn all you can in school."

Larry kicked at a clump of dirt. Luke sounded just like Father.

Luke laid a hand on Larry's shoulder. "Remember when I said about God putting dreams in our hearts?"

Larry nodded. He'd thought about that a lot.

"The Bible also tells us many times that we are to be diligent in our work. That means we're to be responsible, hard workers not slackers. Clyde Bonner was a slacker. He lost his life because of it. If he'd had a passenger, the passenger would have been killed, too. And his plane could have hit someone when he crashed. A man who designs airplanes can't be a slacker without risking lives, either."

Larry bit his bottom lip and kicked again at the clump of dirt. Did Luke think he was a slacker? The thought hurt.

"I know you want to do everything you can to be a good designer and a good pilot," Luke told him. "I don't have any doubt at all that you will do whatever you must to become very good at your work and make your planes as safe as possible."

Larry glanced up at him and smiled. "I will," he promised.

Luke patted his shoulder. "Maybe you'd better find Jack and head back. It isn't good to make your parents too angry with you."

"You can say that again!" Larry took a couple steps toward where he'd last seen Jack. "Oh, no!"

"What?"

"I've lost my books! I must have dropped them somewhere." Larry tried to remember where he could have left them. "I had them when we saw the plane crash. Then we started running. I can't remember if I dropped them then or later. Maybe I left them on the trolley."

"Maybe you better try retracing your steps."

"Yes, but I don't have much hope of finding them. Wouldn't you know I'd lose my books when I've just decided to try to be a better student?" Larry shook his head. "Looks like I'm in trouble again."

CHAPTER 16

The Contest

Larry was glad to find the next morning that a good-hearted trolley driver had returned his books to the school. He'd seen the name of the school stamped in the books. Larry's name was written in the books, too.

Larry had worked with Jack on his assignments the night before, so he had them ready for class.

"Mother and Father weren't even angry with me for going to the crash and losing my books!" he told Jack on the way to school. "They said they understood I needed to see whether Luke had crashed and that anyone might have forgotten his books under the circumstances."

Gloria's day wasn't going as well. Miss Colby had told the

students about the citizenship classes adults were taking. When she found out Gloria's mother and father had taken the classes, she asked Gloria to tell what she knew about them.

In the schoolyard after lunch, Ronald kicked away the ball the girls were playing with.

"Hey! Stop that!" Gloria demanded as Mabel ran after the ball.

"It's stupid for women to think they can learn enough to vote wisely just by taking a few classes," Ronald said, sneering.

Gloria crossed her arms and stuck out her chin. "It isn't stupid!"

"The suffs keep doing stupid things," Ronald said, sticking out his own chin. "Like Prohibition. They think they're so smart, getting that law passed. Did they ever think about the men who'd lose their jobs when people couldn't make or sell liquor anymore?"

"Liquor isn't good for people. It isn't good for kids when their mothers and fathers drink too much."

"You think you know all about it. Do you think it's good for kids when their fathers aren't making any money?"

"Children, children!" Miss Colby stepped in between them. "Let's stop this arguing."

"He said the citizenship classes are stupid," Gloria told her.

"They are!" Ronald yelled.

"Are not!" Gloria yelled back.

"Stop!" Miss Colby yelled.

Ronald and Gloria stared at Miss Colby. They had never heard nice, quiet Miss Colby yell before.

Miss Colby cleared her throat and ran her hands down the sides of her skirt. "That's better."

"You don't think the citizenship classes are stupid, do you, Miss Colby?" Gloria asked, keeping her voice as normal as she could.

"No, but everyone is entitled to their opinion in America, remember?"

"I think we should have a citizenship bee," Gloria declared.

"What's that?" Ronald asked, frowning.

"Yes, what is it?" Miss Colby asked. "I've never heard of one."

"I just made it up. It's like a spelling bee, only instead of asking how words are spelled, the questions are about voting and citizenship and politics and things like that. We could have a suffragist side and an antisuffragist side." Gloria glared at Ronald. "Then we'd find out who knows the most."

Ronald crossed his arms over his chest. "Sounds good to me."

"Well. . ." Miss Colby looked from one to the other. "I guess we'll have a citizenship bee then. Who's going to make up the questions?"

"Why don't you?" Gloria asked her. "You know lots about those things."

"But you're a suffragist, too," Ronald told Miss Colby. "I think Mr. Dilby should make up the questions. He's an anti, like me."

Gloria stamped her foot. "I don't want all the questions made up by some man who is so silly he doesn't think women should vote!"

"Don't call Mr. Dilby silly, Gloria," Miss Colby said. "He is a fine teacher."

Gloria was glad he wasn't her teacher! "Maybe both of you could make up the questions," she suggested. "You can make up half and Mr. Dilby can make up half."

Miss Colby raised her eyebrows. "Sounds fair to me. Does that sound fair to you, Ronald?"

He nodded. "Sounds fair to me."

The bell rang then, and students headed back into the schoolhouse for afternoon classes. Miss Colby grabbed Gloria's arm lightly, holding her back until the other students had passed them and they were alone.

Gloria looked up at her in surprise. Was Miss Colby angry with her?

"When I came up to you and Ronald, I thought I heard him say something about a father not making any money. Is that right?"

Gloria thought a moment. "Oh, yes." She shook her head, remembering his silly argument against Prohibition. "He said that suffragists didn't know what they were doing when they wanted the Prohibition law. He said Prohibition made fathers lose their jobs or something like that. Isn't that silly?"

"It's not silly, Gloria. I think Prohibition is a good thing. A lot of people are mean or irresponsible when they drink too much, and that isn't good for their children. But a lot of people lost jobs when Prohibition became law: people who made liquor, people who sold liquor. One of those people was Ronald's father."

"Oh, my!" Surprise rippled through Gloria.

"This isn't something for you to tell your friends, mind. But maybe if you know, you will understand why Ronald is so angry. His father hasn't been able to get a job that pays as well as what he was doing before Prohibition. The family had to sell their nice house and move into a small flat, where they have only a couple rooms. They had to sell other things, too, like their car."

"And he thinks it's all the suffragists' fault," Gloria said slowly, "even though the suffragists aren't the only ones who wanted Prohibition."

"That's right. Maybe when he's older, Ronald will understand better. We'd best go inside now, before the students send the principal looking for me!"

Even though Ronald made her mad, Gloria couldn't help

feeling sorry for him and his family. She'd never thought before that a good law like Prohibition might hurt someone. She wasn't sure what to think about it.

The next morning Miss Colby told the class that Mr. Dilby had agreed to help make up questions for a citizenship bee. The bee would be held the following Monday. Students could decide which side they wanted to be on.

On Monday, everyone was excited about the citizenship bee. There were more kids on Gloria's team than on Ronald's, but Gloria was surprised at how many were on Ronald's team. Over a third of the class was antisuffrage!

The teams lined up on opposite walls of the classroom. When she looked across the room at Ronald, Gloria remembered what Miss Colby had told her about Ronald and his family and felt sorry for him. *But I want to beat him today, even so!*

"These are the rules," Miss Colby told the class. "I'll ask one question at a time. First one team will be allowed to try to answer it. If they can't or they answer wrong, the other team will be allowed a chance to answer. Only the person I call on will be allowed to answer, but that person can ask the rest of the people on the team what they think. One point will be given for each correct answer. When I've asked all the questions, the team with the most points wins. Does everyone understand?"

She looked from one side of the room to the other, her eyebrows raised.

Ronald's hand shot up. "I think the losing team should have to do something."

Gloria frowned. "That's just like Ronald!" she whispered to Mabel.

"It doesn't matter what he wants," she whispered back, "because we're going to win!" She grinned at Gloria, and Gloria grinned back.

"What do you have in mind, Ronald?" Miss Colby asked.

Ronald crossed his arms and gave Gloria a smug smile. "I think the losing side should hand out flyers that tell the winning side's point of view."

"We agree with that," Gloria said. "It will be fun watching you hand them out, Ronald."

Miss Colby frowned at Gloria but didn't scold her. "As long as both teams agree, that's the way it will be. Now, here's the first question. See if you can answer it, Ronald. What happened at Seneca Falls, New York, in 1848?"

Ronald pulled his eyebrows together and looked at the floor. Some of the other kids on his team whispered answers, and he listened to them. Finally he said, "We aren't sure. Was that where the first baseball game was played?"

Gloria burst out laughing.

Miss Colby looked like she was trying not to smile. "Sorry, Ronald. Do you know, Gloria?"

"The answer is the first Women's Rights Convention."

"Correct."

Gloria smiled broadly at Ronald. He made a face back at her.

"The next question is for Mabel. How does a person mark a ballot when they vote?"

"Um. . ." Mabel looked at Gloria. Gloria leaned over and whispered in her ear. "They mark an *X* in the box next to the name of the person they want to elect," Mabel said.

"Right! Next question for Ronald's team. How many ballots will voters get in the election this November?"

"Oh, I know that!" Gloria whispered to Mabel.

The boy beside Ronald knew, too. "Five."

"Wow! You students know a lot," Miss Colby said. "Let's see if the suffragists can answer this question. What will each of the five ballots be for?"

Gloria and Mabel looked at the next person in their line. It was Arthur, the boy who had been in the debate with Gloria.

Arthur started counting on his fingers. "The white one is for the president and for Minnesota offices. The blue one is for the county officers. The pink ballot is for amendments to the Minnesota Constitution. The red one is for. . .something about pensions. The last one. . .I forget." He looked at Gloria and whispered, "What is it?"

"Uh, it's lavender," she whispered back.

"Lavender," he repeated loudly.

"That's right," Miss Colby encouraged. "What is it for?"

Arthur looked at Gloria. She lifted her shoulders in a shrug. "I can't remember."

Mabel couldn't remember, either, nor could any of their teammates.

Gloria breathed a sigh of relief when Ronald's team didn't know the answer either.

"The lavender ballot is for a question on Minneapolis laws," Miss Colby told them.

Gloria didn't think the question had been fair. *It was really like five questions instead of one,* she thought. But she didn't complain.

"Who is running for president and vice president on the Republican and Democratic tickets in November?" Miss Colby asked Ronald's team.

Now it's their turn for a question with lots of answers, Gloria thought.

The girl with blond braids who had been in the debate with Ronald answered. "For the Republicans, Warren Harding is running for president and Calvin Coolidge for vice president. For the Democrats, James Cox is running for president and Franklin Roosevelt is running for vice president."

"Good!" Miss Colby smiled. "Next question for the suffs. What countries besides America allow women to vote?"

Gloria's team had to work together to come up with the

answers to that question! Their final answer was, "Finland, Norway, Denmark, Sweden, Australia, Austria, Canada, Czechoslovakia, Germany, Hungary, Ireland, Mexico, New Zealand, Poland, Russia, Scotland, and England."

"Correct."

"It sounds like America is way behind the rest of the world, doesn't it, Miss Colby?" Gloria asked.

Miss Colby only smiled. "Next question. Can you name ten of the twelve states that did not ratify the Nineteenth Amendment?"

Ronald's team had to work at that one. They came up with eight of the states almost immediately. "Alabama, Georgia, Louisiana, Mississippi, North Carolina, South Carolina, Florida, and Virginia."

They couldn't remember any others. Gloria heard Ronald say he thought Tennessee was one of them, but the blond girl on his team wouldn't let him say so.

When Miss Colby asked Gloria's team if they knew two more states, Gloria answered right away. "Delaware and Maryland."

"Very good!" Miss Colby beamed.

The game went on for fifteen minutes longer. Both teams won points and missed answers. When it came down to the last question, they were tied.

The question went to Ronald's team. "All forty-eight states have laws saying children must go to school. Which was the last state to pass such a law and in what year?"

Ronald and his team members huddled together, whispering.

Gloria and Mabel grabbed hands and held on tight. "Oh, I hope they don't know! We've just got to win," Gloria whispered. "I couldn't bear it if Ronald won."

CHAPTER 17

The Election

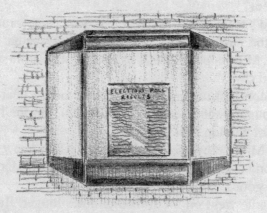

Ronald's team members turned back to face Miss Colby. Ronald took a deep breath. "The last state to pass a law saying children must go to school was Mississippi in 1917."

"I'm sorry, Ronald," Miss Colby said quietly. "That isn't the right answer." She looked at Gloria. "Does your team know the right answer?"

Gloria's best teammates moved close to her. "I know the state," Mabel said.

"So do I," Gloria said, "but I don't know the year."

"I do," said Arthur. "It was 1918."

"Are you sure?" Gloria asked.

Arthur smiled, pushed up his glasses, and nodded.

"All right, here goes everything." Gloria looked at Miss Colby. "It was Missouri in 1918."

"Correct!"

Gloria and Mabel grabbed each other's hands and jumped up and down. "We won! We won!"

The rest of their team clapped and cheered.

Ronald's team wasn't cheering. Ronald was scowling.

Gloria knew she would have felt the same way if her team had lost, but it was hard to feel sorry for him. He always thought he knew everything!

"Ready to hand out flyers for the suffragists?" Arthur called across the room to Ronald. "Or maybe for the League of Women Voters."

Ronald's scowl deepened.

Suddenly Gloria did feel sorry for him. If her team had lost, she wouldn't want to hand out flyers saying women shouldn't have the right to vote.

"Maybe," she started, "maybe Ronald's team could hand out flyers telling people where they can register to vote."

"If that's what you want, that's fine," Miss Colby said.

The antis would still be helping the suffs by handing out flyers, Gloria thought, but at least the flyers weren't actually saying things the antis didn't believe.

When the class sat down again, Gloria looked at Mabel and grinned. Mabel grinned back. They'd won!

"A new job!" Dismay rolled through Larry. "But, Luke, you can't give up flying!"

Luke leaned against *Josephine* and laughed heartily. "I'm not giving up flying. I'll be working with Greg at the Twin Cities Flying Field. I'll be able to keep *Josephine* in a hangar there, which will be much better for her than sitting out in a field."

He patted one of *Josephine*'s lower wings. "A Minnesota winter can be almost as hard on a plane as a war. And it's too cold for sleeping under the wing. I'll still be selling rides on the side."

Larry took a huge breath. "You had me scared for a minute. Hey!" He leaned toward Luke eagerly. "That means you're going to stay in Minneapolis all winter!"

"Yep. Decided I have good friends here. With the new job, *Josephine* will have a good roof over her head. Time to settle down for a while."

"I guess that means you won't need me to run errands for you anymore." He tried not to show how disappointed he felt. He'd been hoping to ask for a special favor in return for those errands, and now he wouldn't have the chance.

"You don't look quite as happy as I hoped you would be to hear I'm sticking around," Luke said with a teasing smile.

"It isn't that," Larry said with a rush.

"I didn't really think it was. Come on. Out with it. What's the problem?"

"You know the election is next week."

Luke nodded.

"Well, Mother has worked really hard so women can vote. So has Gloria."

"And?"

"I thought it would be nice if. . ." Larry told Luke his idea.

"You don't need to do errands for that. It sounds like a great idea! I'll be glad to help out, friend."

When he left the field for home a few minutes later, Larry was grinning. It was good to have a friend like Luke!

On November 2, Larry and Gloria were up before the rest of the family. The day Mother had waited and worked for most of her life was finally here. Election day!

Gloria had talked Larry into helping her surprise their mother with breakfast. Larry wasn't very good at cooking, but he set the table, cut the bread, and poured cold milk. Gloria baked muffins and made coffee, eggs, and bacon. The good smells brought the rest of the family down to the kitchen.

Mother hugged them both. "How nice of you to do this! It's the perfect start to a wonderful day."

Larry noticed that neither Mother nor Father said anything when Gloria cooked the eggs too much. They ate them anyway.

"What time do we go to vote?" Larry asked.

"We're leaving at one-thirty," Mother said. "The city officials have asked women to vote between nine-thirty and eleven-thirty in the morning and two and five in the afternoon."

"Why? What does it matter what time you vote?"

"Most men can't get away from their jobs during those hours and vote. If we women vote during that time, it leaves the trolleys and voting booths less busy when the men need them."

Father set aside his morning newspaper. "I'll be voting when Mother does. I'm going to the hospital this morning to check on a couple patients, but I'll be back to go vote with her this afternoon. We'll all be driving down together. A family affair!"

Larry, Gloria, Harry, and Fred had to wait outside by the car while Mother and Father went inside to vote. For once, Larry didn't mind helping watch his little brothers!

There were other things to watch outside the building. Men and women passed out flyers, urging people to vote for certain candidates. One man wore a board sign, front and back, with the large words painted in black: Vote for Brown!

Harry pointed to him and laughed. "He looks like a sandwich!"

Men who were running for state office stood outside in long, expensive-looking coats, trying to shake the hand of every man who entered the building and tip their hat to every woman.

Larry grinned at Gloria. "They're campaigning up to the last minute. Think they're winning any new votes?"

Gloria looked horrified. "I hope not! Voters should know who they're voting for by now and not change their minds because of a smile and a handshake!"

Larry shook his head, still grinning. Gloria would never change. She always acted like she was a grown-up. But he liked her, anyway.

Luke would like her, too, he thought. *He likes people who are responsible, and Gloria is as responsible as anyone I know.*

When Mother and Father came out of the building, Mother's step bounced.

"You look like the cat who swallowed the cream," Larry told her. "Who did you vote for?"

"Why, Larry, I'm surprised at you! You know that's a secret."

"It doesn't have to be. No one can make you tell if you don't want to, but you can tell people if you wish. Did you vote for Harding and Coolidge or Cox and Roosevelt?"

She gave him a teasing smile. "I'll never tell."

The next stop was downtown. Father parked the car in the middle of Fourth Street, where a row of other cars was already parked.

They entered a large room together. It looked like a banquet hall, filled with tables and chairs where people could sit and talk with each other if they pleased. In the middle of each table was a vase with one yellow flower.

A long table with a white tablecloth at one end of the room was covered with plates of doughnuts, muffins, and coffee cake. A big basket of yellow and white flowers sat in the middle.

On the wall above the table hung the yellow and black banners that were so familiar to Larry and Gloria. "Every Woman a Voter in 1920," the League of Women Voters' slogan, hung in the very middle.

The room was quite filled with people. Men and women milled about or sat in groups at the tables and talked about their favorite candidates. Women from the league walked about with silver coffeepots, refilling people's cups.

Mother started to pull pins from her hat. "I'm going to help serve. The rest of you may help yourself to something if you're hungry. I expect it will become more crowded here as businesses close for the day and more voters stop by. We might need you to help serve then, Gloria and Larry." She hurried off toward the kitchen.

The afternoon seemed long to Larry. People kept drifting in, getting coffee and something to eat, visiting a while, and leaving. About six o'clock, the place began to get very busy.

"Just what are all these people doing here, anyway, Father?" Larry asked.

"Waiting. Most of them have already voted. They want to wait for the results of the election to come in so they know how the people in Minneapolis voted."

"But that takes a long time, doesn't it?"

Father nodded. "Usually takes most of the night, by the time all the votes are counted and people get the news from the polling places to the central counting area. For the entire country, it can take even longer. Each city has to wire their results to the same place, and the votes have to be added up for all the cities and towns."

Just the thought of it made Larry tired.

Mother stopped beside him with a silver coffeepot in her hand. She looked as excited as she had when they came from the voting booth. "Would you like to help us serve, Gloria and Larry? We're getting pretty busy now and expect to get busier as the night goes on. We could use your help."

Normally Larry didn't like to help with things like serving coffee and doughnuts. It seemed too much like women's work.

133

But there were a couple other boys helping who were a little older than he. *Besides,* he thought, *I'm bored just sitting around watching Fred and Harry and talking to Father about the elections.*

For hours, Larry kept busy. He filled silver coffeepots from the big metal pots in the kitchen. He watched the plates on the serving table to make sure that empty plates were replaced with plates full of goodies. He even took his turn doing dishes.

His favorite chore was walking about the large room refilling people's coffee cups. After the polls closed, he was surprised to see a number of the city and state's most important people come into the room. By filling their cups, he had a chance to get close to them.

He tried to keep his hands from shaking when he refilled the governor's cup. It took a lot of courage for him to smile at the man afterward and say, "I hope you win the election, sir."

The governor had beamed back at him. "Thank you, sir."

"Getting tired?" Father asked when Larry filled his cup a few minutes later. Harry and Fred were still with Father. Larry saw that Father had found paper and pencils so they could draw.

"A little tired," Larry admitted, "but it's fun to see all these people. I never thought I'd meet the governor! I recognized him from newspaper pictures."

"I recognized him from the day I went to the capitol with Mother," Gloria said from beside him. She was carrying a coffeepot, too.

"Hello there, gang!"

Larry whirled about. "Uncle Erik! I didn't expect to see you here."

Uncle Erik held up his ever-present pencil and pad of paper. "I go where the news goes."

"I thought today's news was at the voting booths," Larry said.

Uncle Erik grinned. "The women in the league are bringing the news from the polls to everyone today. Didn't your mother show you Hoaglund and Diffendorf's window?"

Larry shook his head. What was Uncle Erik talking about? He looked at Gloria. "Have you seen this window?"

She shook her head. "No." But she wore a huge smile.

"You know something about it," Larry accused. " 'Fess up."

She shook her head again. "You'll have to see it for yourself."

Larry looked at Father. "Do you know about this?"

"It's a mystery to me."

Harry shrugged his shoulders and held out his hands, palms up. "It's a mystery to me, too."

Father grinned. "Let's go see this mystery window."

Gloria and Larry set their coffeepots down on the table.

When they were out on the street, Larry noticed a crowd gathered in front of Hoaglund and Diffendorf's window.

Larry looked at the window in surprise. "Why, there's a screen in the window!"

"There certainly is," Father agreed. "It looks like election returns are being shown on the screen."

"Right the first time," Uncle Erik said, grinning.

Gloria was grinning, too.

"Where are they coming from?" Larry asked. "Where's the projector?"

Uncle Erik pointed across the street.

"Oh, I see. Look, Father, it's in the window of that doctor's office."

"I must say, the League of Women Voters has outdone itself this time, don't you think?" Uncle Erik asked. "It's the first time election results have been given this way to the public—and as soon as the results come in. Sure makes the work easier for us newsboys. And it took the women to think of it!"

"Of course!" Gloria said, grinning.

"How do they get the results so fast?" Larry asked.

"When local polling places finish counting their votes, someone brings the results over here," Uncle Erik explained. "Results from other areas are wired into the Elks Lodge room and brought here. Anyone who wants to come down and watch the window can see what the votes look like without waiting for the newspaper."

"That's why all the candidates and important people are in the league's room," Larry said. "They want to be near the window so they know the results of the election as soon as possible."

Uncle Erik nodded. "That's right."

Larry grinned. "It's rather fun having a mother who's involved with the league, isn't it? We get to meet lots of important people we'd never know otherwise."

Gloria gave him her superior smile. "I thought you said it only made extra work for you with Mother in the league."

"Well, you have to admit, it does that, too. Weren't we just pouring coffee a few minutes ago?"

Gloria laughed. "I guess we were!"

Soon after that, Father took Harry and Fred to Grandmother Allerton's to stay the night. Then he returned and spent the rest of the evening watching the returns and visiting with other men. Mother, Larry, and Gloria worked all night.

"It sounds like Harding and Coolidge have probably won," Father said at dawn as they climbed into the car to go home. "There're still some results that aren't in, so that could change, but it doesn't look likely."

"Good!" Mother said, closing her door.

Larry grinned. "Mother, you voted for Harding and Coolidge, didn't you?"

"I guess I gave myself away! I did vote for them. They represent the same party as President Wilson, and if it weren't for President Wilson's work, the Susan B. Anthony Amendment probably wouldn't have passed at all, let alone in time for women to vote in this election."

Father looked over at her. "Now are you ready to spend more time at home? You've won the right to vote and educated the public about voting and taken citizenship classes. Are you done yet?"

She shook her head. "Why, Mr. Allerton! I'm surprised you ask. We've only begun. Why, in our league committees, we're preparing nine different proposals to submit to the Minnesota legislature. You've no idea how much work needs to be done in areas of child welfare, education, and—"

Father started laughing. Larry and Gloria joined in.

"You're never going to change," Father told her affectionately. "But it sounds to me like the women have changed politics for good."

CHAPTER 18
Larry's Surprise

When the tired Allertons walked into their home, the phone was ringing.

"Probably the hospital." Father hurried across the kitchen, removed the receiver from its hook, and spoke into the mouthpiece. "Dr. Allerton here." He paused.

The family waited quietly to find out who was calling.

"Donald, why are you calling at this hour? Nothing's wrong with Lydia, I hope." Another silence. Father's face broke into a smile. "A girl! Well, congratulations! Yes, yes, of course I'll tell them."

He hung the receiver back on its hook. He was still smiling when he turned to face the family. "Lydia has had a baby girl. Just last night. Donald says both the baby and Lydia are doing fine."

"A baby girl! What is her name?" Mother asked.

"Alice. Alice Lydia Harrington."

"She's only about eighteen months younger than Fred," Mother said. "They'll be able to grow up together."

Gloria plopped into one of the kitchen chairs. Larry wondered if he looked as tired as she did. She closed her eyes and rested her head against the hard chair back.

"Little Alice will never have to fight for the right to vote like we did, will she, Mother?" Gloria asked. "Alice was born with the right to vote."

Mother sighed. "My, that sounds nice. 'Born with the right to vote.' "

Father slipped an arm around her shoulders. "Alice and millions of other women will be born with that right now, all because of the hard work and faith of people like you and Gloria."

Mother smiled. "I think if we don't all get some sleep, we'll be too tired to do any more hard work."

On Saturday after the family had caught up on their sleep and life was almost back to normal, Larry dragged them out to the Twin Cities Flying Field.

"We have seen planes before, Son," Father protested. "Has something new come along we haven't heard about?"

"Remember Luke Harding, the pilot Greg introduced to us at the suffrage parade a year and a half ago?"

"Of course. He's the one you're always going to see."

"Well, he asked me to bring all of you out to the flying field today, special."

Mother looked puzzled. "Whatever for?"

Larry shrugged and looked the other way. He didn't want her to see the excitement in his eyes. "Search me."

When they arrived at the field, Larry led his family over to the hangar where Luke kept *Josephine*. The plane was sitting outside. Luke was checking over his engine.

"Hello, Luke!" Larry called.

Luke turned and waved. "Hello! Just one more nut and bolt to check here, and I'll be with you."

"He takes really good care of his plane," Larry said to Father in a low voice.

A minute later, Luke slid down. He wiped his hands on a rag and put his wrench in his worn leather tool bag before offering his hand to Father.

"I'm glad you were all able to make it. I know your boys well, but I haven't had the honor of getting to know you and your wife and Gloria, though Larry speaks of you often."

Larry could see from the way Father and Mother looked at Luke that they liked the respectful way he was treating them.

Luke rumpled Fred's hair. "This guy has grown a bit since I've seen him last!"

Fred grinned up at him.

"Has Larry told you why he's brought you here today?" Luke asked, looking from Father to Mother.

"No," Father said. "Not really. He only said you asked that we come today."

Luke lifted his eyebrows and looked at Larry. "Do you want to tell them, or should I?"

Larry grinned. "Mother, I wanted to give you something special because of the election and everything. You've worked hard for your dream, and you made it happen. I wanted to give you the best present I could think of to celebrate."

Mother looked puzzled. "Well, that's nice, Larry, but I still don't understand why we are here."

Larry took a deep breath. "I asked Luke to take you and Gloria up in *Josephine*."

Mother clasped a hand to the neck of her wool coat. "You mean up in the air? Flying?" Her eyes grew huge.

"Oh, my," Gloria said in a small voice.

For the first time, Larry wondered whether his mother and Gloria might not *want* to fly. "You. . .you do want to fly, don't you?"

"Well. . ." Mother looked from him to Luke to *Josephine* and back to Larry. "Well. . .I've never thought about it, but. . . yes, of course. It was good of you to arrange it."

"Are you scared, Mother?" he asked. Maybe she was thinking of the four airmail pilots who had died in the last few months and the eight airmail planes that had crashed. The airmail route between Minneapolis and Chicago had been canceled because of all the accidents.

"Well, maybe a little scared," Mother admitted.

"Me, too," Gloria said.

Larry shook his head. "You two talk to all kinds of important people. You speak in front of groups. You fought hard for women's suffrage. I can't believe two people as brave as you are afraid to go up in a plane!"

Luke put a hand on his shoulder. "A lot of people are afraid of flying, Larry. Your mother and Gloria may not wish to go up in *Josephine*."

"Luke takes real good care of *Josephine*," Larry told Mother. "He keeps her in tip-top shape. He's a really good pilot."

Mother took a deep breath. "I want to go. It's a special present from you, Larry, and I thank you for it. It will give me a chance to see why you love flying so much."

Larry grinned at her. "You'll love it!"

"You'll have to take off that hat, Mrs. Allerton," Luke said.

"It's beautiful, but the wind will carry it away if you wear it in the plane. In fact, you should probably put on this helmet."

Larry was proud of the way his mother pulled the soft brown leather helmet over her head without once complaining it would mess her hair.

Luke helped her into the cockpit and fastened her safety belt. Larry helped Luke get the propeller started. Then Mother and Luke were taxiing down the runway, the engine loud in the November air.

The family watched the plane become a speck and then grow large again as it came back to the field. It circled the field low, and Mother waved down at them. Larry waved back eagerly as the plane headed off toward the city.

After awhile, the plane reappeared. Larry could hardly wait to reach the plane after it landed. Luke was already out of his cockpit and helping Mother onto the wing when Larry and Father and Gloria reached the plane. With Luke's help, she slid to the ground.

Her eyes were sparkling. "It was wonderful! Simply wonderful! Gloria, you must try it. Why, it's like looking into forever! I'm so glad you arranged this, Larry. What a wonderful gift! I'll remember it for always!"

"I knew you'd like it."

Gloria didn't look like Mother had convinced her flying was the thing to do, but she slipped on the helmet and goggles Mother handed her and let Luke tighten them for her.

When Luke was ready to help her into the cockpit, Gloria turned and looked at Larry. "This is one of those planes you think is more beautiful than a wedding dress, huh?"

Larry laughed. He'd forgotten he'd said that to her. "It sure is."

"Well, you'd better be right."

"If you don't like it and want to land," Luke told her, "just let me know, and I'll land as soon as possible."

Larry and his family watched them take off. Larry could see Gloria hanging on tight to the edge of the cockpit. He hoped she wouldn't be too scared.

Luke took Gloria over the same route he had taken Mother. Mother chattered away to Father about everything she had seen while they waited for the plane to return.

They all hurried out when the plane landed. Luke lifted Gloria from the bottom wing to the ground.

She pulled off her goggles and helmet and handed them to Luke. "Thank you, Mr. Luke."

"You're welcome."

"Well?" Larry asked. "Did you like it?"

"Wasn't it wonderful?" Mother asked.

Gloria grinned. "It was great! It's the best present I ever had, Larry!"

He took a large breath and let it out. "I knew you'd like it."

Gloria patted *Josephine*'s side. "But, I'm sorry, *Josephine*, I still don't think you're as pretty as Lydia's wedding dress."

There's More!

The American Adventure continues with *Battling the Klan*. The Ku Klux Klan is becoming a strong force in Minneapolis, and Harry Allerton and his cousin Adeline Moe are shocked to discover that it's influencing their friends. When Addy is kind to a Jewish immigrant named Dvora, other girls at school become upset.

Then the two cousins discover a white hood and robe at the house of some friends. Someone they know belongs to the Klan. Who is it?

Harry and Addy learn the Klan member's identity, but they also find out about a Klan plot against Dvora and her uncle. What will they do to stop it?